FAETED UNDER FIRE

Paranormal Investigative Services
Book One

I0630536

Sheri Lyn
Cassidy K. O'Connor

Faeted Under Fire © copyright 2022 Cassidy K. O'Connor, Sheri Lyn

All rights reserved. No part of this book may be reproduced or transmitted in any form or by any means, electronic or mechanical, including photocopying, recording, or by any information storage and retrieval system, without permission in writing from the publisher.

This is a work of fiction. Names, places, characters and incidents are either the product of the author's imagination or are used fictitiously, and any resemblance to any actual persons, living or dead, organizations, events or locales is entirely coincidental.

Celtic Hearts

Press

CHAPTER

One

TRISTAN GROANED as he leaned back in his chair to stretch his back. The long hours sitting at his desk staring at the files were beginning to take a toll on him. Or maybe he was just getting too old for this shit. That was bullshit and he knew it, it was these missing kids making him feel that way.

There had to be something he was overlooking, some clue that would lead him to the culprit, but so far, he'd found nothing. Not a single hair follicle or unexplained fingerprint at any location. He climbed to his feet and headed to the break room for some more coffee. He grumbled as he found the pot empty. "Everybody wants to drink it, but nobody wants to make more." He said loud enough for those still in the other room to hear him.

"Slobs." He muttered as he grabbed a couple of napkins and wiped the counters down, threw away the empty creamer containers, and then leaned against the counter to wait.

"James man, what's up?" A uniformed cop asked as he entered the kitchen.

Tristan nodded, but didn't say anything else. He didn't particularly know this guy other than in passing, and he really didn't care to change that.

"The Lieutenant was looking for you, something about a tip that just came in."

Tristan cocked his head in confusion. "Thanks." He said as he moved past him, forgetting about the coffee as his curiosity got the better of him. None of his cases had a tip line running at the moment, not that that meant they didn't come in. It was just unlikely.

He weaved his way through the desks, and gossiping cops, he stopped outside the Lieutenant's office and tilted his head toward the closed door. "He in?"

The officer stationed outside his office nodded. "But let me check and make sure he's available."

"He was looking for me," Tristan said with a sigh of annoyance.

"Just a minute." The officer knocked and cracked

the door enough to stick his head in. "Yes, sir." The cop closed the door and turned to face him. "He said check your desk. He left the information there for you."

"Oh, for fuck's sake." Tristan stalked to his desk and grabbed the piece of paper. As he read the few lines, he wished he'd waited for the coffee.

> "Tip just came in about the third missing kid. Here's the address. Take Smitty with you, don't go alone!"

Tristan rolled his eyes, glanced around, and called out, "Where's Smitty?"

"Went home." Someone hollered back.

"Of course he did." Tristan dropped into his chair and studied the note, debating what to do. The tip could be shit, and probably was, but that didn't mean he could afford to not check it out on the off chance it was something viable.

Tristan pulled out his phone and typed a quick message to his partner in the unlikely event he was done with court and free to go with him. After ten minutes with no reply, he had his answer. Court was still in session.

He grabbed his badge and gun and went to the

sign-out board. It was this stupid idea of the captains to keep track of everyone. Nine times out of ten, no one even looked at it. But he'd already been written up twice for not doing it and he couldn't afford another one. He grabbed the yellow dry erase marker and smirked as he wrote, "following lead", on the board. They all used it to piss off the powers that be. It was a bitch to erase, and very hard to read at the same time. It was the little things in life, he thought as he made his way out to his car.

Fifteen minutes later, he slowed down as he approached the address he'd been given. The houses were neglected, the grass overgrown with broken toys littering the front yard. He wrinkled his nose at the pungent smell of rot. There was an over-whelming feeling of despair and desperation that overtook him as soon as he stepped out onto the sidewalk. He could feel eyes burning into him, but couldn't see anyone. He knew he wasn't alone, though.

As long as they left him alone, he'd do the same to them. He locked his car, pocketed the keys, and started across the road. The house didn't appear any different from any other one on the street. Every window was either boarded up or had bars across it.

The town's revitalization project had obviously not made it down to this area yet.

He raised his hand to knock, but the door swung open of its own accord. He reached for his gun and held his hand there, ready to grab it, as he studied the dim interior.

"Hello, this is Detective James with the Tampa PD. Is anyone here?"

He hesitated, knowing he shouldn't go in without backup and when his LT or the Cap found out, they'd have his ass. He couldn't hear anything, but that didn't mean shit. Could he afford to walk away and possibly miss the chance of finding out something to help him find those kids?

"Fuck it," He growled as he pulled his gun and eased inside. The interior was just as decrepit as the outside. The smell was a mix of rot, mildew, and dejection. As if even the house had given up on itself.

He picked his way through the debris covered floor, trying to make as little noise as possible as he scanned the room and hallway for any signs of life. A floorboard creaked from behind him. Before he could turn to check, he was tackled, and everything went dark.

Tristan gaped as he saw his body lying in the bed of what could only be a hospital room. The doctors and nurses were talking. He didn't know what most of it meant, but he didn't have to be in medicine to know this was wrong on so many levels. He moved closer to his body and the multitude of scrapes, lacerations, and puncture wounds that littered it.

"What was he attacked by?" someone asked with a tinge of horror etched in her words. "How did he survive to make it to the hospital?"

"We're losing him." One doctor called out.

Tristan's stomach rolled as he watched the hospital staff slowly stop their administrations and step back from his body. He wanted to yell and raise hell, but they couldn't see him or feel him. They'd walked right through him and hadn't even flinched.

He heard a doctor let out a sigh, "Time of death is eighteen thirty-five."

Tristan stumbled backward as his mind whirled and his body revolted. He wasn't sure how he could feel the bile rising in the back of his throat without a physical body, but he felt it. Wasn't your life supposed to flash before your eyes when you were dying? For fuck's sake, where was the white light everyone talked about?

"Doctor. See this." An orderly called out with a hint of hysteria, "He's dead, you said, right?"

"Yes." the doctor replied as he moved back into the room and over to the bedside.

"Then why are his wounds closing like that?"

"His heart is beating... slowly, but it's trying." A nurse called out from where she stood by a monitor.

Tristan yelped as he was sucked back into his body and excruciating pain filled him. He screamed as his body writhed and bucked.

He heard someone call out, "Let's start with Versed 5 milligrams, monitor his breathing, and see if he tolerates that. We can titrate the dose if needed."

"It's not working. Page Dr. Obinski. He was on standby. Tell him I need him here yesterday."

He lost track of time and what was happening after that as the pain consumed him and threatened to drive him mad. It came in waves. He felt like he was burning from the inside. He could feel their cool hands touch him occasionally, but it did nothing to ease the torment.

Suddenly, a new voice filled his ears, overriding

his awareness of the pain for a moment. "Don't fight it. Let it happen and it'll be over soon."

Tristan blinked as he found himself standing beside the bed, staring at his body once again. He felt woozy and a bit disoriented.

"What can you tell me?"

"We don't know much, Dr. Obinski. He was found like this and brought in. He died and then suddenly he didn't." The Doctor huffed out a humorless laugh and shrugged, "He's human, but I can't explain what's happening. This man is healing, and he came back from death."

Dr. Obinski nodded. "No idea what he was attacked by?"

"No." one nurse replied, "No one saw anything. Some kids found him and called it in."

"Well, it would seem somewhere in his genetic makeup there was a shifter. Your human is becoming a paranormal. I can smell ash and an animal on him. As soon as you can release him, we'll have him transferred over to Shifter General." Dr. Obinski said as he turned to face the other doctor. "I hear there are some people here with questions about him. Would you like my assistance in explaining things?"

"That probably won't be a good idea. I can release the patient as soon as you think he's stable enough. In the meantime, I'll deal with them."

Tristan willed his ghostly body to follow the doctor into the hallway where he saw the Chief, captain, lieutenant, his partner, and a couple of other cops waiting.

"I'm Dr. Branson. I've been treating Detective James since he was brought in."

"I'm Chief Bouchard. I'm his commanding officer. Can you tell me how he is?"

"He's stable for the moment. We're not sure what attacked him. From the lacerations and contusions that litter his body; I'd say it was at least a couple of shifters or animals."

"How did he survive it?"

"Frankly, he didn't. We lost him, but he's back now." Dr. Branson paused, licked his lips, and sighed. "I'm sorry to tell you this, but he's being transferred to Shifter General. They will be taking over his care and treatment."

Tristan could hear his coworkers' violent reaction to the news, but he couldn't take his eyes off the devastated look on his partner's face. It matched what he felt inside. He was going to become one of the creatures he despised with every fiber of his being.

The burning sensation he'd felt while in his body started up again and he was pulled backward until he was trapped there, where darkness once again took him under.

CHAPTER
Two

MADDOX SMITH LOVED TAMPA BAY. It was a modge podge of supes and so many of them it was easy to blend in. Even if the humans in this state were the most intolerable of them, he still loved being surrounded by beaches enough to stay.

"Buenos dias, Maddox, I have your coffee here."

Just like he did every morning, he tried to hand the tiny Cuban woman money.

She folded her arms and shook her head. "You know what I'm going to say."

He scowled at her. "We both know you don't mean that glower. I've told you, I'm not the only reason this area is safer now."

"Before you came, this part of Ybor was dangerous. The humans hunted and preyed on us. Now we are left alone and business is better than ever."

He grabbed the cup of Cuban coffee off the counter. "You are so stubborn. Have a good day."

He walked to the end of the line and stopped next to a couple of teenagers. Their wide-eyed stares were almost comical. Even among paranormals, he was considered big. Being part ogre will do that. "She won't take my money. Spend extra on her."

"I see you back there, Maddox. I know you aren't trying to give them money."

He passed off the money as he spun around to look at her. "Of course not. I was asking why they weren't in school."

She shook her head and went back to serving the customer in front of her.

He slid into the driver's seat of his ruby red Dodge Charger, aptly named Scarlet, and gunned the engine as he pulled out. God, he loved his car.

He'd only made it a couple of streets before his peaceful morning was ruined. He slowed down next to the blue minivan and stared at the man in the driver's seat until he pulled away.

The girl on the sidewalk glared at him and turned to storm off. He pulled Scarlet over and chased her down. "Tallie stop."

The girl spun around and scowled at him. "Why can't you leave me alone?"

"Uh, cuz you're sixteen and don't need to be prostituting yourself. What happened to the last shelter I helped you get into?"

Her demeanor changed instantly. She hugged herself and looked at the ground. "There was a guy there that wouldn't leave me alone. I didn't feel safe."

He balled his hands into fists but kept them at his side so he didn't scare her. "I gave you my card. I told you to call me when you needed to."

Her vulnerability vanished. "You're not my dad. I don't need you to save me."

"Relax. It's my job, remember. I could have arrested you ten times over." He pulled out his wallet and handed her sixty dollars. "Get a room for the night at one of the motels on fourth Avenue. There's a big storm coming in overnight and I won't be able to sleep knowing you're out on the street."

"And we both know you need your beauty rest."

When she smiled, she showed how young she was. "Please take the money. Consider it payment for entertaining an old man."

She snorted as she took the money. "What are you, like, fifty or something?"

The old man part had been a joke to get her to

relax. Now he was just offended. "I'm thirty-eight, thank you very much. Now I gotta go. Please get off the street for the night. I'm going to try to find you another place."

She rolled her eyes, but he could see the tears there.

As he drove to the office, he contemplated where he could put a sixteen-year-old pixie and she'd be safe from pervs, both human and paranormal alike, who would love to get their hands on the girl.

His phone vibrated in the cupholder. His stomach dropped as he read the text from his boss, Victor Judge.

> Vic: There's been another kidnapping. Meet me at the crime scene.

He pulled over and waited for the address, then punched it into the GPS and took off.

Another paranormal kid was taken. That made four in five weeks. Whoever was doing it was good. No forensics, no witnesses, nothing that tied the kids together. When he figured out who was doing this, and he would figure it out, he was going to make sure they suffered before they were brought to justice. Kids, runaways, drug addicts, he didn't care. They were all paranormals, and they all mattered to him... or almost all of them did. Faeries could fuck off for all he cared.

CHAPTER
Three

TRISTAN GROANED SOFTLY as he slowly came awake. His eyes fluttered as they attempted to adjust to the bright light. He tried to shield his eyes, but his hands were tied down. He shifted and scowled as he found his legs were restrained as well. He scanned the room for any sign of where he was and what had happened. It was a hospital room, that much he could tell. But something about it was just slightly off from what he was used to.

There was the usual whiteboard with the doctor, nurse, and aide information. A phone number to his room and some other information he really didn't care about at the moment. He turned to his left and could see a hallway that led out of his room. On his right was a chair sitting under a painting.

"Hello, is there anyone out there?" Tristan hollered as he struggled again. Why had they tied him down? Where was he? What was going on?

"Mr. James, I need you to calm down." The nurse said as she rushed into the room. "You're in the hospital recovering from an attack. You need to relax or we'll be forced to sedate you again."

Tristan scowled as he stopped struggling. "Where am I? This isn't the hospital. What is this place?"

"You are in the hospital, Mr. James. I assure you of that. The doctor will be in shortly if you can promise to remain calm. If not, we'll sedate you and try again later when you've had time to rest a bit more."

"I'm fine, I just want some damn answers," Tristan growled out between clenched teeth.

Dr. Obinski came into the room then. "Detective James will be fine, Eloise. I'll take it from here, but thank you."

"Sure, Doctor." She blushed as she rushed out of the room with a giggle that left Tristan really confused.

"I'm sure you don't remember me. You were pretty out of it when we first met." Dr. Obinski pulled the chair closer to the bed and sat down beside him.

"No, I don't."

"What's the last thing you recall?"

Tristan frowned as he cocked his head and lost himself in thought for a minute. "I was at the precinct. I'd grabbed a sandwich from one of the food trucks and just gotten back to my desk. I know I ate it and looked through some reports. But that's the last thing I can remember."

Dr. Obinski nodded. "Good, and do you know what day that was?" He held up his hands. "Don't freak out. I'm just trying to see how far back your block goes. Your memories should return once your mind has processed everything that's happened."

"I feel fine. Why am I here?" Tristan demanded as he pulled at the restraints holding his arm down. "Why am I tied to this god damned bed?"

"Answer my questions and then I'll tell you what I can." The doctor reassured him with his pleasant smile that did little to dispel Tristan's anxiety.

Tristan nodded warily. "Do I have any other choice?"

Dr. Obinski laughed. "Nope, not really. First question, do you have any paranormals in your family tree?"

"Fuck no," Tristan growled as he struggled again. "What does that have to do with anything, anyway?"

"You don't remember being attacked, but you were. You shouldn't have survived it, and to be honest, you didn't."

Tristan froze and stared at the doctor, fear overtaking his body. "How long have I been here? I feel fine."

"We sedated you, but it's been two days since your attack."

Tristan scowled and shook his head. "That's impossible. Is this some sort of sick joke? Fun's over, guys. Let me out of here, you assholes." Tristan yelled loudly.

"I assure you, this is not a joke. You were attacked, you died, you came back and healed yourself. We've had you sedated to give your body some time to adjust."

"Adjust to what?"

"Mr. James, you've got latent paranormal genes. When you were attacked, it reacted somehow and your phoenix rose up. That's the only reason you're still here, alive and feeling so good. He saved you."

"Bullshit. I'm not one of those things. I'm human." Tristan argued. "There has to be another explanation."

"I'm sorry to say there isn't. We did some testing on your blood and it came back with shifter DNA."

"You're one of them too?"

"Yes, you're in Shifter General. The human hospital couldn't take care of you once you'd begun your transformation." Dr. Obinski moved toward the door and looked back over his shoulder. "I can release you from here now that you're awake. Is there anyone I can call to come get you?"

"My partner," Tristan replied angrily.

"I'm sorry, but he refused. Is there anyone else?"

Tristan shook his head no and turned away so he didn't have to see the pity in the doctor's eyes. He was truly fucked now. No one was going to want anything to do with him once they found out.

"Mr. James," the nurse called out as she entered the room. "I just need to check your vitals and have you sign some paperwork and you'll be free to go."

Tristan jerked away as she reached for his arm to wrap the blood pressure cuff around it. He scowled at her. "I'm being discharged. Why do I need this? I just want to go home."

"It's fine. Let him go." Dr. Obinski said with a sigh as he entered the room and passed him some papers. "Take care of yourself, Mr. James. I've included a card to a psychiatrist that may be able to help you with adjusting to your new life as one of us."

Tristan waited for the doctor to put the papers on the bed and then he grabbed them. "Can I go now?"

"I've got some scrubs coming for you to put on. Your clothes were destroyed during the attack. Your personal belongings are in the cabinet beside you. Once you're dressed, you're free to leave with my blessing."

"Thanks," he said gruffly as he climbed off the bed and up to his feet. He half expected to be unsteady or weak, but he felt better than he had in a few years. He pulled the bag out of the cabinet and dumped the contents out. His phone, which was now dead, his wallet, and his watch were all that he had left. He hoped that meant his badge and gun had been picked up by the LT or Cap and not stolen.

"Here you go, Detective James." An orderly announced as the large man placed the clothes on the bed. "Have a nice day."

Tristan waited until the room was empty again before he quickly pulled the scrubs on, grabbed his few possessions, and headed out of the hospital as fast as he could manage.

CHAPTER
Four

MADDOX STARED at the empty twin bed with the stuffed dragon still there, waiting for its owner to come home. "How long has he been missing?"

Vic turned to the younger agent who'd taken the original statements.

The kid nervously flipped through his notebook. "His parents called it in at 8:00 a.m. when they came to wake him for school. I was first on scene at 8:04 a.m."

Maddox glanced at his phone. "So, they have a two-hour head start on us. What's the kid's name?"

"Derek and his parents are Marcus and Gina."

He unclenched his fists and took a deep breath. He had to project confidence, even though he felt anything but that.

Vic clapped him on the back. "This has gone up the food chain. They are talking about sending us resources from the Orlando office. I heard Finneas would lead that team."

Maddox whipped his head to the side so fast he was sure he heard a crack. "I don't want that fucking fae anywhere around here. He's an egotistical prick and he'll just get in the way."

"Finneas has been nothing but nice. You won't even give him a chance because he's fae. Regardless, if you don't want him to come, you need to make some headway. We can't have a fifth victim."

Maddox clenched his jaw as he nodded and walked out. Even if others had already walked the entire house, he always liked to do it too. You could never have too many sets of eyes.

He avoided the living room until the very end, where he found the young parents on the couch, sobbing in each other's arms. "Sir, Ma'am. I'm Senior Special Agent Maddox Smith. I know you've answered a million questions, but do you think you can go over some of it again with me?"

The missing boy's father wiped his face and dried his hands on his jeans. "Yes, of course. I'm Marcus, this is Gina. We just want Derek home, so we'll do whatever you need."

"I understand the last time you saw Derek was when you tucked him into bed last night?"

Gina hiccupped. "I read him a story, gave him a kiss, then shut his door. That was around nine o'clock."

"Have you guys noticed anyone hanging around the neighborhood lately? Or did Derek mention anything out of the ordinary?"

Marcus shook his head. "Almost everyone on this street is a dragon shifter. We look out for each other. Someone would have said something if they'd seen a stranger lurking around."

"Does Derek have any medical conditions or anything we need to know about?"

Gina shook her head. "No, he's perfectly healthy."

"We're going to send some agents to the school to talk to his teacher and classmates. We want to make sure they haven't noticed anyone around who shouldn't have been. You're going to see people coming in and out of here for a while. They are dusting for prints and taking photos." Maddox grabbed a business card out of his wallet. "If you think of anything, call me. I'll check in with you guys in a few hours. In the meantime, Sharon is going to be your point of contact here at the house. She can reach us anytime if needed."

He handed them his card and nodded at Sharon as he walked back to the boy's room.

Vic waved him over to the bedroom window. "There's no sign of forced entry. The mud outside is disturbed, but no footprints. Whoever did this was good. We're not dealing with amateurs."

Maddox poked his head out the window to look at the mud, then stood back up. "There has to be a clue somewhere. With four kids now taken, there has to be something we're missing." He picked up a photo of Derek and his parents. "I hate when it's fucking kids. Why do people have to be assholes?"

Vic patted him on the shoulder. "You're one of my best agents. You're going to figure this out and you're going to bring them all home."

Maddox nodded absently. He wished he had that much confidence. He'd been on the job long enough to know the odds of getting these kids back were slim after the first couple of days. The first kid had been taken three weeks earlier and Tampa had one of the highest rates of human trafficking of any city in the country.

He growled in frustration and set the photo back

down. What were they missing? What's the connection?

He couldn't stand there a minute longer. Normally canvassing was done by the lower agents, but he needed to feel useful. Someone out there had to know something.

CHAPTER
Five

TRISTAN CHECKED his wallet as soon as he exited the hospital front doors. All his cash and credit cards were still there, thank whatever gods were out there for that. He found a bench and sat down as he debated what to do. Should he call a cab or one of those rideshare people? Would they pick him up from there?

"Hey man, you okay?"

Tristan frowned as he realized the valet was speaking to him. "Yeah, I'm fine."

"You've been sitting here awhile. You need me to call you a cab or get a nurse or something?"

"Lost in thought, I'll call for a pickup, don't worry."

The valet nodded and moved back to his

podium. Tristan sighed, pulled out his phone, and ordered a driver to come pick him up. His head was a mess, and he just wanted to get home and relax and try to get his memories back.

"Hey man, is that your ride?" The valet called with a scowl. "Are you sure you're okay?"

Tristan nodded and stood. "Thanks." He replied as he climbed into the car and settled in. It didn't take long to get to his apartment. As soon as they pulled into the parking lot of the complex, he noticed the cops standing around outside. They all gave him weary looks as he climbed out of the car and headed for his apartment. He hoped his roommate was home, since his keys seemed to have disappeared at some point.

"Fucking hell," He grumbled as he noticed the boxes lining the hallway outside his apartment. He tried the doorknob, but it was locked. He knocked and waited. There were faint sounds coming from inside. After what felt like an eternity, his roommate opened the door and leaned against the frame. "What do you want?"

Tristan frowned, "What the fuck, I live here, man. Move and let me in."

"Nope, you used to live here. You've been

removed from the lease, and your shit is packed and ready for you."

Tristan gaped at his former friend until movement behind him caught his attention. "Jason, man. What the hell?" Tristan asked his partner.

"It would've been better if you died," Jason murmured before tossing a set of keys to him. "Your truck is out back. Get your stuff and go. You're dead to us."

Tristan stumbled back in shock, but managed to grab the keys before they fell to the floor. He looked at the stack of boxes and shook his head sadly. "I'm still me, guys. That hasn't changed."

His roommate huffed out a laugh, stepped back, and shut the door. "Fucking hell," Tristan spat out angrily as he grabbed two boxes and headed back outside. He figured he was just lucky they'd packed his shit up and not thrown it out. Hell, they even brought his truck here. They could have left him stranded.

He dropped the first load and turned and froze. "Rookie, what are you doing?"

The cop shrugged as he handed the boxes he was carrying to him. "I have an uncle who was turned, he's still the same guy inside"

"Careful who finds out, they'll turn on you too,"

Tristan warned as they headed back inside. "But thank you."

Once they finished loading his stuff, Tristan climbed into his truck. Next stop was the station and his LT. He needed to get back to work. He needed the stability it would offer in the insane world he'd just found himself stranded in.

The drive to the station was relatively quiet. The never ending traffic in Tampa didn't leave him much time for thinking. For once, he was happy to see the congestion of cars. He pulled into the station lot, parked, and hesitated. "Man up, and face them." He muttered to himself as he climbed out of the car under the intense stare of some uniformed cops. He ignored their hostile looks and their muttered words as he made his way into the station.

Things didn't improve inside as his fellow officers of the law turned their backs, openly glared, or moved so they wouldn't come in contact with him. He felt like he had leprosy the way they all acted. He wasn't contagious, for fuck's sake.

He stopped outside the LT's office and waited for the officer to acknowledge him. He was losing his patience when his lieutenant came out the door and called him inside.

"What are you doing here? You were just released from the damn hospital this morning."

"I'm fine. I was discharged home. I just need to know what happened and what I need to do to get back to work?"

"Fuck, James. You've got to see the Chief, this is .... Fuck, just go see him. Okay."

Tristan's gut flipped as he climbed to his feet. "Thanks, LT."

"Don't fucking thank me."

Tristan turned and headed upstairs to the Chief's office. The secretary outside the door took his name and told him to have a seat. Tristan surveyed the waiting room with a sigh. It was going to be a long fucking day. But at least their chairs looked comfortable enough, and he had a tv to watch the news on.

Four hours later, the secretary finally called his name and gestured for him to go in. Tristan stretched as he stood. He was hungry, tired, and beyond frustrated at the bullshit games. He strode inside and cocked an eyebrow at the portly cop sitting behind the desk. He'd never had much use for him. He'd been a decent cop, but he played the politics game a bit too well for Tristan's liking.

"Detective James." The Chief said with an insincere smile. "Sorry to keep you waiting. I had some pressing matters to handle." He gestured for Tristan to take a chair. "I'll keep this brief. You're no longer human, therefore you no longer have a job on this police force. Your desk is being packed up and you can collect your belongings as you leave."

Tristan gaped at the man in astonishment. "That's it? That's all you have to say? Not even a glad you fucking survived. Just you're fucked, get out and don't come back? I've given this department fifteen years of my life and that's all I get?"

The Chief leaned back in his chair and cocked an eyebrow. "Don't make this harder than it has to be. Leave peacefully before I have you removed."

"What about my case? Who's working it? Have you found anything?"

"Leave, that is police business. You are not privy to that information any longer."

"This is bullshit." He didn't wait to hear any more of the asshole's condescending crap. He climbed to his feet and stormed out of the office. As he neared his desk, he saw the box sitting there filled with his personal belongings. All the files he'd been working on were gone from his desk. He grabbed the box, glared at anyone who looked at him, and headed back to his truck. He'd lost his home, his friends, his job, and his status as a human within the span of a few hours. He climbed into the truck, dropped his head back against the headrest, and laughed. He had nothing left. Maybe they were right and he should have died. It was better than being one of the beings they despised.

A knock on his window startled him. He cracked it enough to hear what the asshole scowling at him wanted.

"You're on police property. You need to leave."

Tristan flicked the man off and rolled his window back up. "Fucking asshole," he muttered as he started his truck and pulled out of the lot. He had no destination in mind, he just lost himself in the routine of driving, as he tried to figure out what to do next.

CHAPTER

MADDOX STARED at the wall of his office. Four pictures of missing kids stared back at him. He'd failed them. He had to find a clue or catch a break soon. He couldn't handle a fifth kid being taken.

His cellphone vibrated on his desk. "Hi Mom."

"Hey sweetie. I hadn't heard from you in a couple of days and I know you were working on a tough case, so I wanted to check in and see how you're doing."

Maddox sighed. "I'm doing better than the four families that still don't have their kids home with them."

"Oh honey, I'm sorry. There was a fourth?"

"Yeah, last night and you know how critical the first couple of days can be."

"Well, I was going to see if you are coming home this weekend for the festival, but this is more important."

Maddox scanned his desk calendar. He'd totally forgotten about the festival, but he also skipped it every year. His mother would never stop asking him though. She just didn't get that he didn't fit in with the ogre community. He hadn't since he hit puberty and his fae wings developed. The fae wings he didn't even know were a possibility since his mom never told him his father was fae.

"Honey, did I lose you?"

He cleared his throat, pushing away the thoughts of the friends he used to have. "I'm here, sorry. Yeah, I can't take any time off right now. Not while there are so many families desperate for answers."

"I get it. I'll tell everyone you said hi, and maybe next week I can drive in and we can meet for lunch?"

"That would be great. Talk to you soon, love you."

"Love you too."

He tossed his phone back on his desk and let out a deep sigh. He really shouldn't shut out the ogre community. His friends had made fun of his fragile looking wings, but they hadn't shunned him. He did that all by himself. He felt like an outsider after that.

"Maddox got a minute." Vic was leaning out of his office across the way.

"Yep, be right there." He grabbed his coffee and sat in the chair across from Vic.

"I got a call from a friend over at Shifter General. There was a cop that had been attacked and basically killed. Lucky for him, he had a latent shifter gene and his animal saved him. The guy has no one now and my friend thought we could use an extra pair of hands."

Maddox rolled his eyes. "The guy was human a few days ago. Just because he shifted doesn't mean he automatically fits in with us."

"You'd rather Finneas come than work with this new shifter?"

That was a low blow. He knew how Maddox felt about the Fae. He hated them almost as much as he hated humans. "Can I get a third choice?"

"These kidnappings have been going on too long. A fresh pair of eyes is a good idea, and I looked up his record. He's been a cop with Tampa PD for fifteen years and has zero complaints against him. For a human, he was a good guy."

"Do I have a choice?"

Vic stood up and grabbed his car keys. "My

friend gave me the guy's cell number, and I tracked him to Wilson's Bar."

Maddox threw his hand up, exasperated. "You just proved my point. What the hell is he doing in a human bar?"

"Give the guy a break. He's been human for the last thirty-six years and now he's got nothing."

Maddox gulped down his coffee and slammed it down on Vic's desk. "Fine, but I'm leaving my dirty cup here."

Vic clapped him on the back as they walked out. "Whatever makes you feel better, man."

Not working with humans and fae would make him feel better, but for the sake of the kids, he was going to have to swallow his pride. Picturing the pretty boy, Finneas, made him shudder. He had to hope the human was the better option.

CHAPTER
Seven

TRISTAN SCOWLED DOWN at the glass in his hand as if it had personally affronted him. "Are you sure you didn't water this whiskey down?" He snapped at the bartender as he walked over to check on him.

"No man, we don't do that shit. And you watched me open the bottle for you. It hasn't left your side. You paid for the whole thing after all."

Tristan grunted as he took another sip and glanced around the bar. Even in his annoyed state, he could recognize how surreal it was to be sitting in the same bar the film Magic Mike was made in. Sexy ass men were in here stripping and possibly sitting where he was now. If he wasn't feeling so fucking sorry for himself, he might actually enjoy being in there.

"Hey man," the bartender interrupted his musings. "That's your second bottle. Why don't you give me your keys? It's not safe to let you drive. I'll even pay for a ride when you're ready."

"I'm not leaving yet, and I'm not even buzzed," Tristan argued as he refilled his glass.

The bartender sighed and moved away, leaving him to wallow in self-pity once again. Even if he did need a ride, he had nowhere to go besides the shitty motel room he'd rented. Luckily, he'd thrown all his crap in there so it wouldn't get stolen out of the back of his truck before he'd come here to drown his sorrows.

The longer he sat, the more pissed off he was getting until the glass in his hand started to heat up and the alcohol boiled.

"Hey man," the bartender called out in annoyance as he pointed to the sign behind him on the wall that read 'no paranormals'. "Your kind isn't allowed in here. You've gotta go."

Tristan scoffed, "You had no problem serving me both bottles, but now I'm not good enough? My money spends as much as yours does."

Two burly men stalked up to him. "Leave before

the bouncers remove you." The bartender demanded as he grabbed the bottle and pulled it away from Tristan.

"Fuck you. I paid for that. When I finish it, I'll leave."

The two bouncers let out a weary sigh as they each grabbed him under one of his arms and pulled him off the barstool. "Let's go, man, don't cause a scene."

Tristan tried to pull his arms free, but they were stronger than him. So much for being a shifter if he couldn't even overpower a couple of humans, he thought angrily, as they dragged him roughly through the bar and pushed him outside.

He spun around and shot the two men a bird. "I want my fucking my money back, you assholes."

They laughed and shut the door in his face. "Fucking bullshit," he yelled as he turned and stopped in his tracks as he saw the two men leaning against a gorgeous red charger staring at him.

The older guy pushed off the car and waved him over.

"What do you want?"

"My name's Victor Judge, and the grouch behind me is Maddox Smith. We're with the Paranormal Investigative Services."

"Paranormal Investigative Services?" Tristan repeated and then let out a small laugh, "You're P.I.S.?"

The brooding guy on the hood snorted. "Told you, boss. That is the dumbest acronym. That's exactly why I won't wear the shirts or hats they give us."

"Don't blame you on that." Tristan agreed, "Now is there something I can help you with or are you just here to hassle me?"

"We heard about what happened to you and thought maybe you'd be interested in a job."

Tristan scoffed, "Oh, so you heard I got kicked out of my apartment, lost my partner, friends, and my job? All because I got attacked, and it unlocked some hidden gene that turned me into a fucking shifter."

The gorgeous brooder nodded and smiled happily. "Yep, that about sums it up."

"Go fuck yourselves," Tristan growled. "I don't work with paranormals." He turned and stormed off, fuming at their audacity. He climbed into his truck and as he backed out, he glanced over to see the two Agents staring at him.

He pulled into the parking spot in front of his motel and climbed out of his truck.

"Hey, we don't want any trouble around here." The manager called out, stopping Tristan in his tracks.

"And you're telling me this why?"

The manager scowled. "Two guys showed up looking for you. They had guns in the back of their pants. They were pounding on your door, shady as hell. Don't be bringing shit here or I'll kick you out."

"I didn't invite anyone, and I don't have any friends looking for me."

"Whatever," The manager turned and headed back inside, mumbling, leaving Tristan to figure out what in the hell the guy was talking about. He looked around but didn't see anyone waiting around, so he unlocked his door and went inside. He had some stuff to figure out, mainly where in the hell he'd gotten this phoenix gene and what he was going to do next. And most importantly, if he did have an animal inside, as the doctor had indicated, how would he know? Would it communicate with him or try and take over? So many questions, and he had no idea how to get the answers he wanted and needed.

CHAPTER
Eight

MADDOX'S EYES WERE BLEARY. No matter how many times he reviewed the files, there was nothing new. The phone on his desk pierced the air with its high-pitched ring. "Hello."

"Hey Maddox, it's Gene. I wanted to let you know all the preliminary test results are in for case three and there's still no forensics. Whoever is doing this is damn good. They aren't new to this."

Maddox's stomach dropped. Was it a serial kidnapper that has been going from state to state, leaving a string of devastated families in their wake? "Thanks, Gene. Let's hope we get something from the most recent case."

"Finger's crossed buddy. Talk to you later."

Maddox slammed the phone down. "Fuck." What was he missing?

Desperate times called for desperate measures. He pulled up the GPS tracking system and found where Tristan was. He grabbed the stack of files and left.

He pulled Scarlet into the shitty motel, almost afraid to leave her there unattended. He stopped in the office and pulled out his badge. "I'm looking for Tristan James. Which room can I find him in?"

The kid shook his head. "So he is going to be trouble. I knew it."

Maddox shook his head quickly. "Not at all. I actually need his help with a case."

The kid's eyes widened. "Is he an agent too?"

"Something like that."

"Well, he's in room four. I saw some food get delivered a bit ago, so he's in there."

Maddox nodded and made his way to the room. He took a deep breath and knocked. Here goes nothing.

Tristan opened the door with a scowl. "What the fuck do you want now?"

"I'm not here for me. Give me five minutes." Tristan stepped back and let him in. Maddox tossed the files on the bed. Several pictures and papers slid out. "I'm here for them."

Tristan grabbed one of the pictures and examined it, before glancing at Maddox and gathering the files. "There's no way." He mumbled as he dropped into the chair at the small table and spread the files back out. "No fucking way."

Maddox slid into the tiny chair and leaned his head back against the wall. Just like he had hoped, Tristan grabbed the notepad and pen off the table and immediately started taking notes.

After ten minutes of silence, Maddox stood up. "I'm going to grab us some coffee. I'll be back in a few."

Tristan absently waved his hand at him in acknowledgment, never looking up from the files.

Maddox mapped the closest paranormal friendly coffee shop and grabbed two larges and drove back to the motel.

He'd left the door lock engaged, so the door was cracked. Not surprisingly, Tristan hadn't moved.

Tristan reached for the coffee and took a sip as he sat back in his chair and studied Maddox. "I've got questions, lots of them. You prepared to answer, or are you going to pull some bureaucratic bullshit line with me?"

"I'll answer everything I can. What do you want to know?"

"First off, how do you keep finding me?"

"One of the perks of being federal and paranormal is we don't have as much red tape as you guys do. We tracked your cell phone to find you at the bar, and then I put a tracker on your truck before you came out. You know, just in case you tried to jump from a bridge or something for being a disgusting paranormal now."

Tristan shrugged, "Can't deny the possibility didn't cross my mind." He paused, took a sip of his coffee, and sighed. "Is there anything you withheld from me in these files?"

"These aren't complete files. I brought the summaries. I have a ton more data back at the office. This was just to see if you were interested."

"I don't want to be. I want nothing to do with you, your agency, or the paranormal race in general, if I'm being honest."

"I hate to break it to you, sugarplum, but you're one of us now. So you can wallow away in this piss poor motel, feeling sorry for yourself. Or you can accept your reality and do some good."

"Only because it's kids. They're innocent, and I can't stand by and not help them if I can."

Maddox would never admit it out loud, but he was relieved. He needed the help whether he wanted it or not. "So, does that mean you're in?"

Tristan groaned and rubbed his hands down his face. "Fuck." He met Maddox's eyes and nodded. "I'm in."

Maddox stood up and held his hand out. More as a test to see if the other man would touch him. "Welcome to P.I.S. You start at nine a.m. tomorrow." He turned back before walking out the door. "Oh, and that human alcohol isn't going to do shit for you anymore."

"Fuck," Tristan growled loudly.

Maddox laughed the entire way back to his car. Maybe having this guy around was going to be more entertaining than annoying. Either way, it'd be fun to annoy him. For the first time in weeks, he had hope that they might actually solve this case.

CHAPTER
Nine

TRISTAN GROANED as his alarm beeped and woke him from the dream he was having. He was torn between excited to work and terrified of being side by side with all the creatures that went bump in the night. His phone beeped with an incoming text message. He grabbed his phone from the nightstand and opened the message.

Maddox: Morning, forgot to give you the address. I'll drop you a pin. See you at 9 sharp.

Tristan: I didn't give you my phone number, asshole.

Maddox: Fed, remember, we do what we want.

Tristan laughed and put the phone down so he could get ready. He believed in doing a good job, even if it wasn't where he wanted to be.

Twenty minutes later, he was out the door, a nasty cup of instant coffee in hand, heading to his first day. With any luck, they'd have decent coffee. Otherwise, he'd have to rethink this whole idea.

He pulled into the agency parking lot with a couple of minutes to spare. He sat there and studied the building and the people coming and going as he tried to gather his courage to go inside.

His phone beeped with another text message. He grabbed his phone and tried not to laugh at the smart ass message.

> Maddox: I can see you're here. Get your ass inside we can start the day.

Tristan grabbed his backpack and headed toward the front door, where a smiling Vic stood waiting for him.

"Glad you made it. You're right on time."

"Thanks." He mumbled as he moved past the older man.

"I'll give you the fifty-cent tour on the way to

Maddox and your new office," Vic explained as they started down the hallway.

Everyone they passed smiled and welcomed him. Tristan's scowl only deepened the farther they went through the building. He couldn't figure out what to make of these people. It was almost stepford how friendly they all were.

"This is your pod. There are eight agents assigned to each one. Your unit is your family and your backup. The strengths and weaknesses are balanced out, to make each group as powerful and successful as possible."

Tristan nodded he understood as he took it all in. The middle of the room consisted of a large table with ten chairs, a white board hung at one end with a podium in front of it. Around the outside of the room were five doors leading into offices and a sixth into a break room.

"Each team of two agents is given one office to share, but a divider can be erected as needed for privacy." Vic continued on as he motioned for Tristan to follow him down the hallway on the right. "This will be your office."

Tristan peaked in the offices they passed. The agents that noticed all waved hello or called out a greeting. "Excuse me, Sir. What do I call you?"

"Sir, Judge or ASAC, which means assistant special agent in charge, in case you didn't know. Any of those three will work."

"Sir, is it normal for ..." Tristan gestured around the room with a shrug,

"What for them to let their true forms out?" Vic filled in for him.

"Yeah, basically."

"Yes, they aren't ashamed of who they are," Vic explained as he knocked on Maddox's door and pushed it open.

Inside, Maddox stood in front of a wall filled with the pictures of the missing kids with information taped up next to each one. A flash of heat shot through him as he watched Maddox lean forward to read something. His ass was shown off to perfection in the form fitting blue jeans he was wearing. What he wouldn't give for him to turn around and show him how well they cupped him from the front as well.

Tristan shook his head at his wayward thoughts. Where in the hell had that come from? He didn't lust after paranormals.

"Maddox, your new partner is here," Vic called out, getting Maddox's attention. "Tristan, this is your desk. Coffee and vending machines are in the break room. Maddox will give you a better tour when you're ready. We have a cafeteria that serves high-quality food down on the third floor, if you're interested as well."

Maddox turned and nodded at him. "Morning. I put the detailed files on your desk and logged you into the forensics system so you can get caught up."

Tristan nodded his thanks and sat down. He was a bit overwhelmed and was happy for something to focus on that wasn't his new teammate. Time passed as he examined the files and made notes and jotted down questions he wanted to look into later.

"Hi, I hope I'm not interrupting anything too important?"

"Uh," Tristan stammered as he took in the woman standing next to him. She was gorgeous, with her dark red hair and purple eyes. But the horns on the top of her head were really throwing him off.

"I'm Raelle," she set a cup of coffee on his desk with a smile. "I wanted to welcome you to the team."

Tristan swallowed audibly. "Um thanks." He said as he used one finger to push the cup of coffee to the edge of his desk. He didn't know what she was, and wasn't sure he wanted to know. She gave off some type of energy that was making him question things he hadn't questioned since he was a teenager and first discovered how much he liked boys.

She glanced at Maddox questioningly, then shrugged and walked out.

Maddox chuckled. "You get used to her effects after a while. She really had me questioning things a lot in the beginning."

Tristan nodded in agreement. He hadn't been sure which way Maddox had swung before now. Guess that made things easier. It was one less thing he had to worry about being hassled for.

"You really should try the coffee." Maddox interrupted his thoughts. "It's Hell's Brew. It's made for paranormals, and it's like nothing you've ever had before."

Tristan stared at the cup and slowly reached out for it. It smelled delicious, and he really needed the caffeine. He brought it to his mouth and took a tentative sip. "Fuck me,"

Maddox laughed, "Told you."

Maybe working here wouldn't be so bad if they had more of this coffee. "Can I buy this stuff somewhere? I need more of it in my life."

"We have it shipped in from a paranormal town up in Massachusetts. I don't think it's in the stores around here. Speaking of that, when you get settled somewhere more permanent, I can point out the best paranormal restaurants and stores."

Tristan frowned as he realized the truth of that statement. The world as he knew it was gone. Everything had to change. But Maddox had one thing right. He needed to find some place to stay besides the shitty ass motel he was in. Especially if random people were looking for him for unknown reasons.

Maddox stood up and stretched. "A bunch of us are going for Cuban sandwiches if you want to go?"

"I'm here for the kids, not to make friends."

"Suit yourself. It doesn't hurt me if you don't eat."

Tristan watched as Maddox left the office and met up with the rest of the team. They laughed and joked as they left the office together. He almost regretted turning them down, but he just wasn't comfortable being around them yet. He'd seen a side of paranormals that left a lingering fear in the back of his mind. Humans couldn't protect themselves against the more powerful race of beings. It'd left them at a disadvantage for too long. He'd been to too many crime scenes where these monsters had left everlasting scars. Logically, he knew people were just as evil, but in his experience, their kind preyed on those weaker than them.

CHAPTER

Ten

MADDOX HAD no interest in befriending Tristan, but he knew what it felt like to not fit in. He dropped a bag on the new guy's desk. "Brought you a pastry. If you are done with the files, we can walk through the board?"

"Why would you do that?"

"It was a welcome to the team thing. No big deal."

Tristan grabbed the bag and pulled the pastry out with a nod of thanks. "Yeah, let's talk about the cases. There's something I want to bring up, but I want to see what you have to say about your missing kids first and see if it fits in anywhere."

Maddox walked over and pointed at the first picture. "This is Logan Burns. Eleven-year-old octopus shifter. On Sunday, March 13th, he was at the skatepark where he rides all the time. Parents called and reported him missing after he didn't come home at the agreed upon time."

He took a step to the right and pointed to the next picture. "On Saturday, March 19th, nine-year-old Aurora Massey, who is a sprite, went missing while riding her bike in the neighborhood."

"Monday, April 2nd, thirteen-year-old Daria Nixon, who's a vampire, was at soccer practice after school, but when her dad showed up to pick her up, she was gone."

"Yesterday, seven-year-old dragon shifter Derek Rowland was taken sometime in the middle of the night from his bedroom. His parents tucked him in for bed and the next morning they found him gone."

He stepped back and leaned against his desk. "Different ages, different paranormal types, different times of the day, and days of the week. I can't find a pattern."

Tristan leaned back in his chair and nibbled on his pastry with a frown of concentration. "Before I was attacked, I'd been working on some cases of missing kids. Four, to be exact. My memories are a bit fuzzy and my files were confiscated, but I think we need to look into it. The ages and dates are sticking out for some reason."

Rage filled Maddox. There was a string of human kids going missing and they didn't know about it? He stomped over to the office door. "Vic, do you have a minute?"

He stepped back and chewed his nail as he tried to calm himself down. He knew the human and paranormal forces didn't really talk or work together, but how did both sides miss this?

Vic came in and leaned against the doorjamb. "You know, the agent usually comes to the boss, not the other way around."

Maddox gave him a droll look but chose to ignore him. He turned to Tristan. "Want to tell him?"

"I think we need to figure out how to get the Tampa PD to work with us, or at least share files. I was working on a string of missing kids before I was jumped and left for dead. Four kids similar in age and taken in close proximity to your dates. I can't be sure without their reports how close. But there is something nagging at me that they are connected."

Vic cursed under his breath. "We've been trying to get the Governor to agree to a shared database for years, but they've refused."

Maddox shook his head in disgust. "They probably don't want to see how much human on paranormal crime there is. They'd rather pretend it doesn't happen."

Tristan cocked his head and frowned. "We'll come back to that in a moment. I have questions. The Chief was a good cop, but an even better politician. He rose in the ranks quickly, but I don't recall there ever being any reports of him abusing his powers against either side. He may work with us, but I don't think the request can come from me. We didn't part on good terms. He threw me out, if I'm being honest."

"So, he's a good cop, but he threw you out?" Vic questioned skeptically. "Sounds like he's got something against you or paranormals, if you ask me."

Tristan shrugged, "I don't know. I'm not his biggest fan, but until yesterday I'd never had an issue with him, per se. Is he a bigoted asshole, maybe... I really don't know for sure anymore."

Vic stared at the board for a second. "Okay, let me give him a call and see if he wants to create a joint task force. Or if nothing else, at least send over the files for us to compare."

Maddox snorted. "Good luck with that. There's no way they are going to agree to work with us."

"Well, pigs can fly, so you never know. I'll keep you posted."

Tristan gaped, "What the fuck? There really are flying pigs?"

Vic chuckled. "Maddox, you have a lot to get him caught up on. Good luck with that."

Maddox glared at the other man's back as he left. This is exactly what he didn't want. He wasn't taking on a baby supe. "Why don't we go visit the crime scenes so you can see what we're working with?"

"Sure, but first I need one very important question answered before I'm leaving this office."

"Oh, this is gonna be good. What's your question?"

"Do I get a gun and badge? I'm an official P.I.S. Agent, right? Or at least a gun, so I'm not completely defenseless out there."

Maddox leaned forward and clapped his hands with each word he said. "You... are... paranormal." He shook his head, annoyed. "You have powers now. We can get your gun and badge from Vic before we go, but you really need to get comfortable using your powers too. There are a thousand ways to take down a supe without a gun being one of them."

"Powers, that until you just told me I didn't even know I had. They are going to be great for me to use.

Do I just close my eyes and pray they work or something? Give me a fucking break here. I was human a few days ago. I don't understand any of this bullshit."

"Have you even tried connecting to your phoenix yet? Have you spread your wings at all? Mine are usually itching to get out when I'm home."

"What the fuck? I have wings? Wait, you have wings too? And how the hell do I connect to my phoenix?" Tristan closed his eyes and groaned, "I feel a massive headache coming on."

Maddox took a deep breath. "You're right. That was a lot too quickly. You're my first human convert too, so I forget everything that is normal to me is alien to you."

"Ten more and you get your toaster then?"

Maddox bit the inside of his cheek. He wasn't going to reward him with a laugh. "I'll work on finding someone who can come in and help you, but in the meantime, let's get your stuff and go."

"Sure, drop a bombshell and then say let's go. Fucking asshole."

Maddox grabbed his stuff and led Tristan across the pod.

Vic was on the phone, his face red. He pushed a button on the phone and held it away from his ear.

"I'm on hold. Fuckers keep transferring me around. What do you need?"

"The hatchling here," he pointed over his shoulder to Tristan. "Wants a gun and badge. Then we're going to drive to the crime scenes."

"Fucking asslicker," Tristan grumbled softly.

The pod erupted in laughter. Tristan spun around to see everyone watching them.

Maddox patted him on the shoulder. "Super hearing, remember. You might as well give up on whispering from now on."

Maddox laughed loudly at the look of frustration on Tristan's face. Maybe this wasn't going to be so bad. After all, he couldn't remember the last time he laughed. He leaned close to Tristan. "And for the record, you'd be lucky if I did."

He turned and grabbed the gun and badge Vic was holding out and handed them over to Tristan.

"No, don't transfer me again. God damn it."

Maddox stepped past Tristan. "Let's get out of here before he fries another phone."

"Did you say fries them?"

CHAPTER

Eleven

TRISTAN FOLLOWED MADDOX IN SHOCK. What in the hell had he gotten himself into? A boss that fried phones, a partner who was built like a brick shit house and had wings. Plus, a fucking sarcastic mouth that rivaled his own. And a team that could hear everything he said, no matter how quietly he said it. He was definitely not in Kansas anymore, that was for sure.

"Let's take Scarlet for a ride."

"Uh, I think you got the wrong idea about me here. I don't do women in any form."

Maddox spun around, his jaw dropped. "How dare you talk about Scarlet that way? She is a lady."

Tristan glanced around in confusion, "Wait, just

who the hell is Scarlet, anyway? Are you... Do you..."
He trailed off and frowned. He didn't care, he didn't
need to know this man's preferences.

Maddox swung his arm wide and pointed to his
Charger. "That is Scarlet, you hornball."

Tristan stared and licked his lips. "I'd love to get
my hands on her. If I beg, can I take her for a ride?"

Maddox snorted. "No one can handle Scarlet's
curves like I can. It will never happen. Now get in the
passenger seat and don't drool on her."

"No promises." Tristan scoffed as he hurried over
to the beautiful car and carefully eased onto the
black leather seats with a sigh. "She's so soft and
warm. This might be as close to heaven as I've ever
come in a woman."

Maddox laughed as he peeled out of the parking
lot. They drove for a few minutes in silence as
Tristan took in the sights. They were in a part of
town that catered to the paranormal races. As a
human, he'd never come down to the area. He
wouldn't have felt comfortable or welcome.

Tristan sat up as Maddox pulled over and put the
car in park. "Stay here. I'll be right back. Don't touch
anything."

"Ass." Tristan grumbled as he watched Maddox

climb out of the car and give him a glare of warning before walking down the street a few dozen feet and stopping in front of a teenage girl.

Maddox threw his hands up and then grabbed his wallet and pulled out a wad of cash. The girl shook her head and then reluctantly took the money and walked away. Tristan frowned as he tried to figure out what the hell had just happened. Why had Maddox paid the kid off like that? Was he paying her off or buying drugs?

After a few minutes of Maddox staring after the girl, he turned and headed back to the car. He climbed in and pulled Scarlet back into traffic without a word of explanation.

"You gonna explain what I just saw?" Tristan finally asked after the silence became too heavy. "Cause I gotta admit that didn't look very good."

"Not sure what you are implying. I'm helping my community, that's all."

"That's not vague at all," Tristan grumbled. "Helping how? I don't work with crooked cops, so if you're into illegal shit, I want out now."

Maddox's hands gripped the steering wheel before he finally sighed. "Her name is Tallie. She's a sixteen-year-old sprite that ran away from an abusive father. She sells herself to survive. I've gotten her into a couple of shelters, but she always leaves again. When I see her, I give her money to get off the street for the night. One day I'll find a permanent place for her, but for now, this is all I can do." He turned and glared at Tristan. "There, does that satisfy your curiosity?"

Tristan shrugged, "Can't blame me for asking, man. It looked fucking suspicious as hell. I think it's naïve as hell, but I can't blame you for trying to help her."

"I know what it's like to have nowhere to go and I have money to spare. If that's naïve, then that's fine with me."

Tristan frowned, but didn't push Maddox for more information. It wasn't his place, and he really didn't care. At least he didn't want to care. Maddox's past had nothing to do with the case and why he was there. If the man was lonely, that was his problem. His only focus needed to be on this case and finding the kids. His partner was a grown-ass adult who could handle his life on his own.

"Where are we going first?" Tristan asked once the silence had grown awkward again. Or maybe that was just Tristan's own insecurities. Silence gave him too much time to think, and he wasn't ready to be left in his own head just yet.

"We're going to start at the beginning and go in order. I'm not taking you inside the newest victim's house yet. Those parents are a wreck and the agents who are social workers are still helping them through the process."

"Seeing the locations where they were taken from is good enough for now. Maybe I'll see something that you guys wouldn't have thought of. A different perspective as a former human, I mean."

Tristan cringed as he heard the words that came from his mouth. He hadn't meant for them to sound quite so elitist.

"I'll let you in on a secret. If I hadn't brought you on the case, they were going to bring over this fucking idiot Fae from the Orlando office. So, in all honesty, I'll take every perspective you have."

Tristan itched to ask questions, hell at this point he could fill a couple of notebooks with all the questions he had, but he didn't want to get involved in Maddox's life any more than he had too. This case was all he needed to focus on, not the gorgeous giant next to him.

"Hey, you never answered my question earlier." Tristan paused and glanced at Maddox. "You asked if

I'd even tried to connect with my phoenix. How... is..." He trailed off with a nervous laugh. "I'm not even sure what I'm trying to ask, to be honest. I'm a bit overwhelmed by it all."

"I don't have an animal inside me. I'm not that kind of supe. I know you have to connect with it, but I don't know exactly how you do it. I would imagine meditating or getting really drunk and focusing on it would work."

"Wait, I can still get drunk? I thought you said I couldn't?"

"Remember how we have that really strong coffee... we also have alcohol made just for us. It would probably kill a normal human after one drink."

Tristan stared openmouthed, "And this shit is safe for us to drink? Even me?"

"Totally safe. If you are scared to try it on your own the first time, we can grab dinner and test it out? Unless you want to go back to that shit motel for take out again?"

"No, thanks." Tristan replied quickly, with a frown. "I think the motel and food are about all I'm ready for at the moment."

He saw Maddox's shoulders tense. "Whatever

man. I was just offering to be nice. You do whatever you want."

Part of Tristan wanted to hate himself for turning the other man down, but the logical side of himself said he was doing the right thing. He may have transformed into a paranormal, but he didn't know shit yet and that made him as useless as a human.

CHAPTER

Twelve

MADDOX HELD the door for Logan Jacks. Tristan was already glued to his computer monitor. "Enough of that already. Vic said he's still working his channels to get the task force and or files. I brought you a present." He pointed at the burly guy next to him that was one of the few men in the office who was even close to his size. "Logan here is a bear shifter. We're going down to the training area on the first floor and he's going to work with you on connecting to your animal."

Tristan's eyes bulged as he took in the large man standing in the door and nodded. "Uh, hey man." He turned and looked at Maddox, "I didn't bring anything to work out in this morning."

Maddox smiled ruefully, "Don't worry. We have a

ton of clothes down there covered in P.I.S. you can use. You can take a bunch home with you, too."

"Your sense of humor leaves something to be desired," Tristan replied as he climbed to his feet and offered his hand to Logan in greeting.

Maddox didn't miss that Tristan actually was offering to touch the other paranormal.

"It's nice to meet you, man." Maddox had never had a thing for Logan, but his deep gravelly voice always affected him.

Tristan visibly shivered and then offered a smile, "So, you're going to be like my Obi Won then, big guy?"

Heat rushed Maddox's face. What the fuck. How did mister I hate paranormals switch to flirting with one? He was suddenly regretting bringing Logan in. He should have found some weasel or badger shifter. They're always puny. He cleared his throat. "Should we go?"

He led them down to the gym and handed Tristan a pair of shorts and a t-shirt. "They don't have sneakers here, so you are going to have to go barefoot."

"We're trying to teach me to connect to my phoenix. Why do I need gym clothes?"

"Until Vic calls, we have time, so we're going to

do some sparring, too. But more importantly, a lot of shifters shred their clothes when they shift. Since we don't know what your animal looks like, you might want to keep your clothes safely in your locker."

"Wait," Tristan interjected as he looked Logan up and down. "Your clothes will get shredded when you shift. So when you turn back to human, you'll be naked?"

Logan and Maddox exchanged glances and laughed loudly. Logan nodded. "You'll learn very fast our kind has no problem with being naked around each other. It's totally natural, so we don't think anything of it."

Tristan raised his hand, "Former human here, what about .... What happens if... you know... we get ... um... turned on.... That's kinda hard to hide if we're naked."

Maddox shrugged. "Shit happens. We don't really think anything of it. It does make it easier to know if someone's attracted to you, though."

"Okay, well, I guess that's one way to look at it. It's going to take me a bit of time to adjust to this new way of thinking. Humans have always been a bit more ... prudish about their nakedness. And as long as I'm not going to get my ass kicked for waving my interest around, then I can learn to deal."

"Don't worry, your ass is safe... for now." He pointed to a door across the room. "If you prefer privacy, you can go change in the locker room. We'll wait here for you."

"What if I don't want it to be," Tristan mumbled as he headed toward the locker room.

Once Tristan was out of sight, Logan turned to Maddox. "So, you two got a thing, or can I throw my hat in the ring?"

Maddox's stomach rolled. How did he answer that? Tristan was his own person. If he wanted Logan, Maddox wouldn't stop him. But he couldn't ignore that he was having very unpartnerlike thoughts about him. The dream he'd had the night before was downright pornographic. "He's barely tolerating paranormals right now. In fact, you're the first one he's touched since the change." That was a sobering fact for Maddox. Did he take that as a sign that Tristan was interested in Logan?

They stopped talking when they heard the locker room door open and close again. Maddox had guessed what size to give Tristan, then gave him a size smaller. Boy, was he glad he had.

"I think next time I need bigger shorts. I feel like I'm going to be circumcised by these things."

All three men shivered at the thought as they all reached down and covered their junk.

"You ready for me to shift?" Logan asked as he grabbed the edge of his shirt and pulled it over his head. "I don't want you to fear the change, so I thought if you could see what it looked like, it might help you."

Tristan nodded as he licked his lips. "Yeah, that's good." He agreed quickly.

Logan smirked as he pulled his shorts down, eyes staying glued to Tristan's as he kicked them away so he was standing there in all his glory. "To shift, I just focus on my animal and let him take over."

Tristan gasped and stumbled backward with a quick glance to Maddox as Logan's form shimmered and transformed into that of a giant brown bear. "Holy fucking shit."

Maddox nodded approvingly. "I haven't seen your animal in a while. I forgot how big you are."

"That's what he said." Tristan agreed with a laugh.

The bear roared as it nodded.

Maddox moved back as Logan stepped toward Tristan and planted his giant paws on Tristan's chest. The force knocked him on his ass.

Maddox walked over and squatted next to Tristan. "Shifters come in all shapes and sizes. Imagine if he was actually trying to hurt you."

Tristan struggled and cursed as he fought his way free. He stumbled backward, shaking. "I don't have to imagine shit. I've seen what you guys can do. I've seen the devastation and damage firsthand."

Maddox felt like shit. He should have thought about Tristan possibly having PTSD from the attack. Even though he said he didn't remember it, didn't mean subconsciously it wasn't there.

Logan immediately shifted back and pulled on his clothes. "I'm sorry, man. I was just having fun."

Tristan wiped the sweat from his brow and frowned. "Have you ever seen what your kind can do to a human?"

Maddox's jaw tightened. "Have you ever seen what your old kind can do to a shifter?"

"How can a human possibly hurt a shifter? We've got nothing on your strength, speed, and abilities. You prey on the weak humans and laugh as they get hurt."

"First of all, not all shifters are giant bears. I've seen a group of human boys take a seventeen-year-old nymph and torture her for days. Paranormals are not all-powerful beings. Second, stop saying 'we' like you are a human still. You're a fucking paranormal now, so deal with it."

"Fuck you," Tristan screamed in frustration. "I'm trying, okay. This isn't easy for me. I lost my whole fucking life in a span of a few hours. I'm trying to adjust and accept my new reality. But come on, what do you expect me to do when a seven-foot bear tackled me." Tristan leaned against the wall and slowly sank to the floor with his elbows on his knees. "Logically, I know there are monsters on both sides, but I've rarely seen anything but the bad and it starts to warp things, you know."

Logan held his hands up to shut them up. "You both forget this all started with the rift between our realms. Neither side confessed to creating it, but it took both to try and fix it. The explosion caused damage to both humans and paranormals that were still being felt three generations later. Our worlds collided that day and forever changed our ways of life. We've been trying to coexist on this new joint plane of existence and there are going to be growing pains. You can't go from what we were as two separate entities to what we have now, humans with paranormal genes, supes with vulnerabilities. Things that shouldn't be possible are happening every day."

Maddox stared at Logan, stunned. The gruff guy had never been so eloquent before. "Damn, when did you get so smart?"

Logan reached down and held a hand out to help Tristan up. "There's more to me than just my good looks and charm. So shallow." He winked at Maddox.

Logan patted his stomach. "The downside to shifting is it takes a lot of energy. I need food asap. You guys coming?"

Maddox glanced at Tristan, wanting him to make the decision.

Tristan shook his head. "I'm going to shower and get changed. I need a minute. I'll catch you guys after lunch."

Maddox felt bad leaving him. He didn't look good, but it was obvious he wanted to be alone. "Alright, we'll see you after."

There was a rock in the pit of his stomach as he walked away. He had rushed Tristan too fast. Why was he always such a fuck up?

CHAPTER
Thirteen

TRISTAN WAITED until the vending machine room was empty and headed inside to grab a sandwich from the machine. It wasn't that great, but it'll do. He had too much on his mind to be around others just yet. He dropped the sandwich on his desk and booted his computer back up. He needed to see if what Maddox had said was true. Was there really that much violence from humans against Supes? And if so, why had he never heard of it? Shouldn't the Tampa PD be involved in those types of cases?

He'd only gone back a decade and the amount of hate crimes he'd pulled up was astonishing. He'd been on the force that whole time, yet he knew nothing about any of these cases.

"You still look like shit. Do you want to take the afternoon off?" Maddox leaned against the door-jamb, studying him.

"I've been doing some research and I just can't wrap my head around it. How has this been kept hidden for so long?" Tristan gestured to the computer and the case file he had pulled up. "Hundreds of reports of humans attacking paranormals, hundreds, man."

"Don't beat yourself up. We are kept separate. We live in silos and it's hurting all of us."

"Do you think the powers that be encourage it for some reason? Can they gain something from keeping us divided? I can't justify it and it's fucking with me, bad."

Maddox shrugged. "I really hadn't given it any thought. I don't see why they'd be doing it purposely. I really think it's just the natural way of things. This hatred between our kinds is generations old. It's what we're all taught. Maybe we just didn't know better?"

Tristan frowned as he pushed himself away from the computer. "I need some air."

"You know what always makes me feel better? A cup of Hell's Brew and stretching my wings. Why don't we go up to the roof and see if we can get your wings to come out?"

"I'll settle for coffee, but right now, I'm thinking that the liquor you mentioned sounds even better." Tristan smiled as they headed out of the office to grab a cup and then up to the roof. "You know I still don't know how to connect to my phoenix, so what makes you think I can get to my wings?"

"I'm not saying you will, but we're still waiting on Vic, and the latest forensics reports aren't back yet, so let's just try."

Tristan nodded and followed behind Maddox. He was starting to really enjoy following his partner around if it meant he got to watch his fine ass. They reached the roof, set the drinks down, and faced each other.

"So, how do we do this?"

Maddox shrugged. "I'm not sure how it works for you. For me, I can feel my wings under my skin. It gets itchy if I don't let them out to stretch." He walked around Tristan and brushed the area between his shoulder blades. "I feel it here. Concentrate on that part of your body. Try to connect with them. They are a part of you. You should be able to sense them."

Tristan felt like an idiot as he turned his attention inward and tried to feel what Maddox was describing. The only thing he could pick out was the heat of his hand on his back. It was distracting as fuck. "Dude, help me out here. Can you show me how you do it?"

Maddox stepped back and crossed his arms against his chest. Tristan turned to watch him. Maddox shook his head. "I don't show anyone my wings."

Tristan frowned and nodded. He wasn't going to push. He could hear the inner turmoil in his tone. "Okay, uh I can try again, I guess. It's just hard when I'm working blind here."

Tristan dropped to the ground to sit down so he could concentrate. He focused his thoughts and energies on his back, to what he'd imagined it would feel like to have the wind caress them like it did his hair. After a few minutes, he sighed and opened his eyes. "I got nothing here."

Maddox's jaw clenched several times as he stared at Tristan. "Fine, I'll show you, but if you laugh, I will throw you off this roof and if your wings haven't come out, I will let you hit the ground."

Tristan nodded seriously, "don't know why you'd think I'd laugh. I've been sitting here like a fucking idiot for the last twenty minutes. Earlier, I embarrassed myself in front of you and Logan. I think I've got the cap on vulnerability right now."

Maddox sighed heavily, then yanked his shirt over his head and threw it on the ground. He turned around so Tristan could see his back.

Tristan gulped as he took in the sculpted naked back standing in front of him, damn that man was drool worthy. He jumped as Maddox's wings suddenly appeared. "Holy shit." He whispered in awe as he climbed to his feet. "They are fucking amazing. Can I touch them?"

"Full disclosure. Touching my wing is arousing, so I'll do my best to not react."

Tristan nodded and slowly reached out. "They're beautiful, almost silky feeling and the colors are magical. So many shades of blues. They look so delicate, but they must be strong as hell since they have to carry you. This is incredible." Tristan shivered as he felt Maddox do the same. "Why do you hide them?"

Maddox hung his head but didn't turn around. "You want my dirty little secret? My mother is an ogre. That's where I get my size from. She had a one-night stand with a guy. It turned out he was Fae."

"Yeah, and what's so wrong about that?"

Maddox spun around. "A big ass ogre with feminine fairy wings. Ogres made fun of me for them, and when my dad showed up and wanted to be a part of my life, the Fae community wanted nothing to do with me. They are conceited assholes who think I'm too brutish and ugly to be a part of them."

"Full disclosure," Tristan growled as he moved to stand in front of Maddox, "I think you're fucking gorgeous, with your wings and as huge as you are. If they can't see that, then it's on them. Don't take this the wrong way, but you made me hard as hell when you did that."

"I appreciate the gesture, but you don't have to lie. I know exactly what I look like." Maddox bent down and grabbed his shirt. He pulled it over his head angrily. "The second this shift is over, I'm going to have a drink. This has been a fucking miserable day."

"Would it be okay if I tagged along? I think I need something to take the edge off the last couple of days."

"Suit yourself. You can follow me to Tanner's on 8th." He strode past Tristan.

Tristan sighed and followed him. He hadn't been lying about anything he'd said. But he knew better than to try and convince him. Hell, he was still coming to terms with the fact he was lusting after a paranormal.

He laughed softly. Who'd have thought that on day two of his new life, he'd be in this position?

CHAPTER
Fourteen

MADDOX HELD the door of Tanner's open and waved Tristan inside. "I know it's your first time in our kind of bar. I promise no one bites unless you ask them to."

"That's never been one of my kinks." Tristan replied with a smirk.

"Yo, Maddox, I got your bar stool open for you." Maddox waved at the bartender and led Tristan across the room. "Who's your friend?"

Maddox slid on the stool. "Froggy meet Tristan. He just joined the agency." Maddox leaned forward. "He's never had paranormal alcohol before." Froggy's eyebrows popped up. "Yeah, I know, but we do have to work tomorrow so we won't get too crazy."

"Take it you come here a lot?" Tristan said as he took in the bar.

Maddox shrugged as he glanced around. "Maybe once a week."

"Ha!" Froggy shook his head. "I think you're here more than you are at work."

Tristan cocked an eyebrow. "Is my new partner a functioning alcoholic? Or are you trolling for sex?"

Maddox didn't want to admit it was neither. He was in here most nights because he was so fucking lonely at home he couldn't stand it. When he wasn't here, he was driving the streets just patrolling, but his wallet could only take so much of that. There were too many supes that needed help. "Neither, it's the mixed nuts." He held up the bowl on the bar. "These things are addictive." His stomach rolled at the idea of actually touching the shit that was probably a germ infested cesspool.

"You like salty nuts, got it." Tristan laughed and faced Froggy. "What do you suggest for my first drink?"

"Depends on what you like. Tell me what human alcohol you drank and I'll make you something you'll love."

Tristan bit his lip, cocked his head, and then smiled, "Dragonberry rum's pretty good." Tristan scowled, "Wait, that isn't made ... like from you guys, is it?"

Maddox kept a straight face as he nodded solemnly. "They milk the dragons to get the alcohol. It's a very dangerous job, but you've tasted it. It's incredible."

"For fuck's sake," Tristan gaped, "That's not what I meant, asshole."

Froggy burst into laughter and shook his head at them. "No, that was just some human's idea of a good name. It's strawberry rum, so explain to me how they got dragon anything, out of that."

Tristan shrugged, "People are weird, what can I say. I stopped expecting normal out of them a long time ago. It's made my life a whole lot easier that way."

Froggy grabbed a black bottle from under the counter. "Well, if you like the fruit-flavored stuff, I'll make you a *Crusty Sunburn*."

"Uh, not sure I want anything crusty going anywhere near my mouth, thank you very much."

Maddox rolled his eyes. "Such a spoilsport. Come on, you're a supe now. Time to experience the real stuff." He looked back at Froggy. "Make it two."

They sat silently, watching their drinks get poured. Maddox had never actually had whatever this drink was, but he didn't want Tristan to know that. He agreed the name was disgusting.

They grabbed their cups that had faint wisps of smoke coming out of the top and turned toward the room. "So, want to play darts or pool or just people watch as we get buzzed?"

"Pool sounds good, if you're up for it."

Maddox led them toward the corner where the pool table was. "So question, you seem really comfortable here. I expected you to be nervous, eyes darting all around."

Tristan shrugged, "I don't know. I kinda thought I would be too, but then I walked in here and it's pretty much like every other bar I'd ever been to. It's comfortable and familiar, I guess you'd say."

"Hey whatever works. After the day you had, it's good you get some down time. And it's good for you to see we're normal people, that do normal stuff just like you and your human buddies did."

"From the sounds of it, you don't do this. You just sit at the bar and drink." Tristan winked as he gathered the balls to rack them.

"I eat the peanuts, not drink, and it's not all the time." Maddox grumbled as he glared toward Froggy. Dude made him sound like a drunk.

Tristan laughed, "If you say so, man." He lined

up to take his shot. "You mentioned your parents, but what about siblings?"

Maddox stared at the table as he watched the balls break. "It was just me and mom until I hit puberty and my wings came in. Mom admitted what my dad was and called him to come talk to me about my changing body. Why she thought bringing in a complete stranger at such an awkward point in my life was a good idea made zero sense."

"Wait, your mom had a one-night stand and, like thirteen years later, she still knew how to contact him? Maybe she felt a bit more for him than she ever admitted to you."

Maddox leaned over and aimed his stick at the cue ball. "One night during an argument with my father about him leaving us, he admitted he had asked mom to marry him but she turned him down. He tried every so often to get back with her and she just kept him at arm's length."

"Shit, man. That sucks hairy asshole." Tristan moved around the table, trying to find a good shot.

"Thanks for that visual, didn't need that."

"I've learned it grosses just about everyone out. You have like a 99.9 percent chance of it working."

Maddox fist pumped the air as he got two more balls in the pocket. "Mission accomplished on grossing me out. Now what about you? Please tell me your family is as fucked up as mine?" Maddox's face fell. "Oh my god, do they even know you transformed yet? Did they tell you where the gene came from?" He knew he was throwing a lot at him, but it just dawned on him.

Tristan sighed, "It's just my mom and me. Just after I graduated high school, my father died in the line of duty. My paternal grandparents died before I was born. My mom's mom was adopted and had my mom while she was in high school. The father didn't stick around. It's just been the two of us for a while now." Tristan frowned as he studied the table. "She's got early onset dementia. She knows I was attacked. But I don't think she really remembers it, you know."

"Damn, you win for worse family problems. At least I still have both my parents, so I really can't complain."

"My mom was amazing though. She had my back and always tried to take care of those around her. I wouldn't have traded a minute of my life with her for anything. And she still has good days, and they just started a new trial drug that sounded promising."

Froggy walked up with two more drinks. "You guys don't even look like you're feeling the crusty sunburns, so here's *Succubus Milk*. If this doesn't get you going, I'm not sure anything will." He handed one of the drinks to Tristan and then gave Maddox a look. "Your groupie paid for yours."

Maddox blew out a breath and glanced around. Dustin, a guy he had spent one night with, was sitting at the bar, staring at them. He waved at Maddox.

Tristan glanced over to see what they were staring at. "Who's your friend?"

"He's not a friend," Maddox growled.

The bartender patted his back. "If you'd stop being so good in bed, maybe they'd stop hanging around here begging for more." He glanced over at Tristan. "Your pal here doesn't do attachments, and he always manages to find the hookups that end up wanting more."

Tristan cocked his head and studied the other man and shrugged, "I don't see the appeal at all, but to each their own. Maybe we should start vetting your bedmates for potential stalker tendencies."

"Oh my god, both of you just stop. Once in a while I go on dates. It's no big deal."

"Pfft." The bartender shook his head as he started walking away. "No one here actually believes that you date them before sleeping with them. It's okay man. You do you."

"I think the word you're looking for is cruising." Tristan winked.

If Maddox could magically disappear, he would. He wasn't ashamed about his habit, but it still didn't feel good to be made fun of for it.

Maddox held his head in his hands. The Succubus Milk and other four drinks they had really did a number on Tristan. Maddox spent the last hour dragging Tristan away from every patron in the bar. Apparently, his research that morning had gotten to him. He felt the need to hug every one of them and say he was sorry. Maddox wasn't sure what he had to apologize to them for, but he needed to do it from a safe distance and not inches from their faces while spitting as he said every word.

The door to the bar opened, four more people came inside. Tristan saw them at the same time Maddox did. "Shit." He had to distract him. "It's getting late. Why don't we get going? We've got to work in the morning, right?"

"Aye aye, sir." Tristan giggled as he smiled at Maddox. "Let me just find my keys."

"Don't bother. I took those from you two hours ago. I'm driving you home and I'll come back for you in the morning. With the amount you've drunk, you'll probably still be inebriated tomorrow."

"Were you trying to play pocket pool with me? If you were, I'm sorry I didn't notice."

Maddox rolled his eyes as he grabbed Tristan's arm and led him to the car. "I'm sure you would have loved that." He opened the passenger door and stopped short. "If you puke in Scarlet, I promise your transition will be the least painful experience of your life. Got it?"

Tristan gasped in horror, "I'd never do that to such a classy lady. Besides, I don't get sick from alcohol. I can't even tell you the last time I was hungover."

"Mmm-hmmm. Let's see what you think tomorrow morning."

Maddox shut the door and ran around to the driver's side. He was going to drive slower than a ninety-year-old on the way to the bingo hall. He was not risking this newbie getting sick.

Tristan rolled his head on the headrest until he was facing Maddox. "I'm drunk, but I really mean it when I say you've got beautiful eyes and a nice, firm ass." He hiccupped and then laughed uncontrollably.

Maddox didn't want to laugh, but he couldn't help it. If only he'd been recording Tristan. He'd have enough mortifying blackmail to last a decade.

Would Tristan still think he had a nice, firm ass when he was sober?

"Where are we going again?" Tristan asked with a yawn, "I don't think I want any more to drink tonight."

"You're not going anywhere else. It's off to bed for you. Vic will have my ass if you call out already because of me."

"Wait," Tristan exclaimed as he sat up and stared at Maddox, wide-eyed. "I'm not one of your floozies."

"You are going to bed alone, asshole. How easy do you think I am?"

Tristan giggled, "You really want me to answer that? I saw the guy in the bar, remember? He wasn't someone I'd boast about sleeping with."

"Ouch. You're a judgmental prick when you're drunk, aren't you? Dustin is a perfectly nice guy." Maddox prayed Tristan wouldn't remember any of this tomorrow.

"Maybe, but he was only good for scratching an

itch." Tristan shrugged. "He's just not the forever type that you need."

"And I suppose after a few days, you think you know so well what my forever type is?"

"Maybe not, but I know for certain it wasn't him. He was too needy for you, he wouldn't let you be you, and he definitely wouldn't challenge you. That's what you need, someone to call you out and stand up to you when you're being a stubborn douche."

"With our job, don't you think having someone docile at home would be a good thing? I think we get enough challenges day in and day out." Maddox didn't know why he was arguing with Tristan. If he just stayed quiet for a minute, the other man would be passed out. But his words were triggering and for some stupid reason he wanted Tristan to understand him.

Tristan shook his head fervently and then grabbed his head. "That was stupid." He grumbled softly. "And no, I don't think so. You'd be bored off your fine ass within a week and then you'd be out trolling for someone to give you what you need. A partner, not a doormat."

Maddox would die before admitting Tristan was right. Thankfully, he didn't have to worry about it as he pulled into the parking lot of the motel. He parked in the spot in front of Tristan's room. "Okay Princess, you're home."

Maddox bit back a laugh as he watched Tristan struggle to sit up and find the door handle. As soon as he did, Maddox pushed the lock on the door. He waited for Tristan to curse, then he unlocked the door. "Geez Tristan, it's not that hard to work a door."

"It keeps locking and unlocking. I don't think Scarlet wants me to go."

Maddox waited for Tristan to try the handle again and hit the lock button again.

"Motherfucker. Would you help me, please?"

It took every ounce of restraint to keep a straight face as he walked around and opened the door for him. "I told you it wasn't very hard."

Tristan yelped as he tumbled halfway out the door before Maddox caught him. "Shit. I was leaning on that."

Maddox sighed. "Are you going to be able to get yourself inside?"

"I can do it, I think. Just point me in the right direction."

"We're literally right in front of your door. You just have to walk ten steps forward."

Tristan nodded, "Oh." He groaned loudly as he

tried to pull himself up. He flopped back down in the seat, then pulled himself up again. "Ha, got it." His legs wobbled for a second before giving out again.

"Oh for fuck's sake." Maddox bent down and lifted him onto his shoulder in a fireman's hold. "Got your room key? I'll spin you around so you can open it."

"Fuck me, you're strong. That's so hot. Bet you can manhandle me in bed, can't you?" Tristan hiccupped and then laughed. "Oh, don't spin me too fast. I might vomit down your back otherwise."

"Paranormals can be killed. I suggest you not throw up on me or you'll be the next missing body." Maddox shivered. He hated vomit. If he even heard it, let alone smelled it, he would throw up too and with the amount of alcohol they had, that wouldn't be pretty.

Tristan squirmed on his shoulder. Maddox didn't even think about it. He reached up and smacked his ass. "Stop moving."

Tristan let out a needy moan and then gasped as he felt something rip through his back. "Fuck me, what was that?"

Maddox sputtered as he pulled feathers out of

his mouth. "Your wings just popped out and they're hitting me in the face."

"My wings?" Tristan repeated in shock. "What do they look like? Put me down so I can see."

Maddox bent down and set Tristan on his feet. He grabbed the room key from his hand and opened the door. "Let's get inside at least. There are mirrors in there."

Tristan stumbled inside and beelined it to the bathroom mirror. "Holy shit." He gasped as he turned sideways to get a better look at his wings. "They look like fire. That's so fucking awesome."

Maddox was relieved. With how hard Tristan had been taking the transition, he had secretly been worried the other man would reject his wings once he saw them protruding from his back. "They look fierce. You're going to have no problem flying."

"They're sexy too." Tristan grinned. "I'm not too sure about the flying thing yet, though. These things will really support my weight and keep me in the air?"

Maddox shivered and let his wings pop up. "If these flimsy things can carry my big ass, yours definitely will carry you."

"Flimsy my ass, they are gorgeous and contrast

with your size perfectly." Tristan shrugged his shoulders and smiled. "Move, please."

Maddox folded his wings back in and stepped to the side. Unsure what Tristan was planning to do.

Tristan laughed as he jumped up on one of the beds and moved to the edge. He crouched down and leapt into the air, only to crash face first onto the nasty motel carpet.

"You're such an idiot." He laughed as he leaned down to help Tristan up. "You didn't really think that was going to work, did you?"

"I thought I was human a few days ago, too." Tristan shrugged sheepishly. "And it sounded good in my head, anyway."

"Why don't you put those away for the night and we can try again tomorrow when you're sober?" Maddox tried to push him toward the bed.

"How do I do that? It's not like I know how to control them. Hell, I'm not even sure what made them come out this time." Tristan blushed and glanced around. "Well, I do, but not sure that's going to help put them away."

"And when we're out on the street chasing a perp, I can't smack your ass every time I need you to fly." although, Maddox liked the thought.

Tristan shivered. "Fine. How do you make yours come and go so easily?"

"I just focus on the center of my back and will them to go in and out and it works. I've been doing it for almost twenty years."

"In and out." Tristan groaned and shook his head. "Damn it, why is everything so sexual with you?"

"Or you're just a perv," Maddox smirked at the incredulous look on Tristan's face.

Tristan dropped on the edge of the bed and closed his eyes. "Just will them away." He mumbled softly as he concentrated.

Gusts of wind blew around the room as Tristan's wings beat feverishly. "That's the opposite of putting them away."

"I'm trying, but it feels so cool to feel them moving and the air caressing the feathers. I see what you meant earlier. It must be so erotic to have them be stroked."

"Definitely a perv." He chuckled to take the sting out. "Are you going to put them away and get in bed or what?"

"Can I just sleep like this and hope they go back inside?"

Tristan unceremoniously turned and flopped

face down on the bed. His wings fluttered a few more times before settling against his back. Within seconds, he was out cold and snoring lightly.

"He is going to be so mortified tomorrow if he remembers any of this."

Maddox pulled the blanket over him and shut off the lights before leaving. As he reached for the door handle, there was a loud knock. He opened the door to two large men looking shocked to see him.

"Oh sorry, wrong room."

Maddox nodded and watched them turn and leave. Instead of going to another room, they got in their car and left. "What the fuck?"

He glanced back at Tristan. Had he planned a booty call and forgot about it when he got drunk?

Not that Maddox had any room to judge. He never slept with the same man twice, but he'd never taken on two guys at once. Maybe there was more to Tristan than Maddox first thought. Maybe his new partner wasn't the narrow-minded bore he thought he was.

CHAPTER
Fifteen

TRISTAN GROANED as the knocking got louder. He rolled over in bed and glared at the door. "I'm coming. Hold on." He yelled as loudly as he dared. He climbed out of bed and sat there for a moment to let his body adjust to the new position. "Fucking hell." He grumbled as he stood up slowly and made his way to the door.

"What?" he demanded as he pulled it open to a smirking Maddox. "What are you doing here so early?"

"Making sure you got up for work. I told you last night you weren't missing today."

Tristan flicked him off, but accepted the large cup of coffee he held out to him. "Thanks. Let me get a shower and change."

Maddox laughed, "Sure, figured you need it." He closed the door and moved to sit at the table. "So how much do you remember of last night, anyway?"

Tristan shrugged as he grabbed some clothes and moved into the bathroom. He hadn't had time to even think about what had gone down yet. His head was throbbing and his mouth felt like cotton had invaded and taken root.

"You've got fifteen minutes." Maddox hollered from the other room, leaving Tristan to growl in frustration. The only thing he wanted to do was take a long, hot shower to wash the lingering alcohol that was seeping from his pores. As he waited for the water to adjust to the temperature, he thought about what he could recall.

"Did my wings really come out?" He called out suddenly. "Holy crap, they did, didn't they?"

Maddox laughed, "Yup, who would have thought a bit of pain would be your trigger? They came out, and you even tried to fly.... Well, of sorts."

Tristan groaned as more of the night came back to him. It would seem he'd gone from keeping Maddox at arm's length to making lewd comments and suggestions. He felt his face flame as he thought about the bar and the other patrons. If he never went back there, it would be too soon.

Vic stood in the center of the pod with the rest of the team. "Glad you guys could make it."

Maddox pulled out a chair and sat backward in it. "Car trouble."

"Is that why you two rode in together today?" Cole called out with a waggle of his eyebrows.

Maddox rolled his eyes. "Tristan, have you met the rest of the team?"

Tristan glanced around and nodded to Raelle. "No, just my coffee mate there," He said with a smile.

Raelle laughed, "Good stuff, isn't it?"

"Yeah, I might be addicted now." He held up the large cup he was holding in salute.

One by one, they went around the room and introduced themselves. Next to Raelle was Cross. Cole stood next to his partner, Reed. Sitting on the other side of the table were Jasmina and Kiely and Ensley and Shephard.

"There are pods on every floor so we can always pull in extra help if needed, but for the most part, this is your family," Vic said, then started flipping through a file folder.

Tristan raised his hand and waited.

Vic cocked his eyebrow. "You don't have to do that or wait to be called on. This isn't school."

Tristan shrugged, "Sorry, didn't know the protocol. My question though is Maddox only said we do these meetings a couple times a week, but not exactly what they are for."

Maddox sighed, "You weren't listening to me more likely. Each team consists of ten agents. We work in groups of two, but have our pod and, if needed, other teams to call upon for help. These meetings are for each set of agents to bring everyone up to date on their cases and get feedback and help. Some members of this team have skills that can be utilized by all of us."

Tristan nodded, "So it's like a round table. Everyone helps everyone. That's pretty smart."

Vic smiled. "Glad you think so. It helps so that if a pair needs help, we all know the basics of each other's cases, too. And on that note, the family of Maddox's latest kidnapping is holding a vigil this afternoon. They are walking from his house down to the park and lighting candles. If no one has anything pressing, I'd like as many of us out there as possible. Not only to look for suspicious activity but also to show the community we do care. Pressure is really mounting for us to solve this, so it's all hands on deck."

"Have you had any success getting those files?" Tristan asked after a moment. "I think these cases are too coincidental to be anything but connected. We've got to figure out a way to work together."

Cross scoffed. "You remember how you felt walking in here a couple of days ago. So what makes you think humans will work with us?"

Tristan shrugged, "I think that for some reason, both sides are kept in the dark about a lot of things. Don't we have a PR team that can try to help bridge the gap? There are some human cops that don't hate us, right?"

"Not enough," Cross grumbled and turned his attention back to Vic.

"He's right, sadly enough." Vic sighed. "But you're right. We've allowed ourselves to stay segregated and if this case has shown us nothing else, we have common enemies. Working together can only benefit us and just maybe the next generation will grow up united as one."

"Sir." Tristan licked his lips as he thought about how he wanted to say what was on his mind without coming across as a total asshole. "Most of the superior officers in the TPD are not very open-minded.

They come from a different time, I guess. But you're different…"

Vic smiled. "I won't take offense." Vic ensured him. "You want to know why I agree with you?"

Tristan nodded, "Basically yes."

"I was born as a human. I was turned while I was in high school. Almost everyone shunned me. But my girlfriend stayed by my side and supported me, and she's still there even now."

Tristan's mouth fell open in shock as he replayed his words over in his head, what kind of love they must have for her to stick around through that and while they were teenagers. That was a level of love he couldn't even fathom.

"But to answer your question about the files, I'm still being jacked around. I haven't given up, though."

"If you want, I might have some contacts over there who will still work with me. I can go through unofficial channels and see if I can get them."

Vic nodded. "I'll let you know. Let's give them another day or so, and then you can go through the back door."

Tristan couldn't help the snicker that escaped at Vic's words. Maddox sighed and elbowed Tristan. "Can you stop thinking about sex for two minutes?"

Tristan shrugged, "Sorry, not sorry." He grinned as he turned his attention to the unit as they began to fill everyone in on what they were working on.

"So, how does this work, exactly?" Tristan asked as they stood outside the latest victim's house.

Maddox scanned the crowd as he took off his jacket. "We are going to stand back and let them gather. We'll spread out and follow them down to the park, looking for anyone that doesn't fit in. Sometimes humans come around to disrupt our funerals and stuff, so we want to make sure the vigil is peaceful. We need to wear our gear just in case."

He reached in the trunk of Scarlet and handed Tristan a vest and grabbed one for himself.

Tristan pulled his on and zipped it up. He frowned as he looked at Maddox's and then down to his own. "What the hell, man?"

"I made it very clear that I am not wearing anything with that acronym on it. I had this special made." Maddox smiled proudly, showing off his vest with Paranormal Investigative Services spelled out.

"Fucking hell," Tristan grumbled. "Why didn't you tell me that was an option? I don't want to walk around with P.I.S. all over me either." When he got back to their office, he was filing a complaint or buying his own or whatever he had to do to make sure he never had to put this shit on again. Some fucking partner Maddox was turning out to be the asshole traitor.

"You are still on probation, low man on the totem pole has to put up with the bullshit."

Tristan walked away grumbling, "I'll show you low man on the pole."

The front door opened, and the family stepped out with sad smiles. They thanked everyone for coming as they led the crowd down the sidewalk towards Derek's favorite park. Tristan scanned their surroundings as they walked. He couldn't imagine what the family had to be going through, but he was happy to see such a good turnout. It didn't help them find the kid, but with luck, it would give the family a bit of hope to know people cared.

Once they'd reached the gazebo set close to the playground Derek loved, they stopped and gathered around. He had to tune out the father as he climbed the podium to deliver his plea for the safe return of their son, while the boy's mother sobbed behind him in the arms of a family member. The line of people waiting to speak grew steadily as Tristan watched. It was going to be a long, emotional day.

Maddox tossed his vest in the trunk of Scarlet. "I'm going to Tanner's for a drink. I need to forget the last couple of hours. Want to come?"

Tristan paled at the thought. "Uh, thanks, but I think I'll pass. The smell from outside earlier when we picked up my truck was enough to tell me I'm not ready for another drink just yet."

"No problem, I've had those days, too. Get some rest and I'll see you in the morning."

"Later," Tristan called as he climbed into his truck and headed back to the motel. He really needed to figure out some place to stay permanently. This worked for now, but he really needed a place of his own. He pulled into the parking spot and groaned as he saw the manager making a beeline for him.

"Those guys were back, and they were talking to another man in a car. This place isn't the most upstanding, but these people give me the creeps big time. I wrote down a description of all three of them and the car this time. Don't know if it'll help you or not, though."

Tristan frowned and accepted the paper. "Did they say anything?"

"Not really, asked if you were in. They knocked on your door and then went to the other car and talked to the third guy. After a few minutes, they all left, and that was the end of it."

"Thanks." Tristan called as he headed to his room, lost in thought. Who could be looking for him, and why? Could these be the guys who'd attacked him?

As he opened the door, he looked over his shoulder to make sure he was alone. He shut the door and flopped down onto his bed with a sigh. He grabbed the remote and flipped through the channels for a few minutes before turning it off and giving up. He was too restless to sit still. He grabbed his keys and headed out to Tanners.

He pulled into the parking lot, turned off his truck, and debated the wisdom of going inside. He figured as long as he didn't have more than a drink or two, he'd be fine. As he was approaching the front door, he saw Maddox exit with his arm around a guy. He froze in place as he watched them head to Scarlet. He knew he was being irrational, but he hated seeing some random guy going off with his partner.

Maddox reached for his car door and glanced up.

Their eyes met across the parking lot. He wasn't sure which one of them looked more surprised. Tristan turned with a curse and climbed back into his truck. Maddox could do what he wanted with who he wanted, but that didn't mean he was going to stick around and watch it happen.

He could hear Maddox calling him, but he pulled out and didn't look back. He got back to the motel and jumped out of his truck.

Tires screeched behind him as Scarlet pulled into the next spot over. Maddox jumped out. "Tristan, why'd you take off?"

"Why did you come after me? You had your fun picked out for the night. There wasn't any reason for me to be there."

"Don't make it sound like that. Today was rough. I couldn't go home and be alone and you turned me down. I need to get my emotions out somehow." Maddox shouted.

"Join a fucking gym, or go for a run. There are a thousand things you can do besides pick up rando's at a bar to get your rocks off with." Tristan turned and unlocked his door with a growl of frustration.

Maddox grabbed his arm and pulled him around. "Why do you care what I do in my spare time?"

"I don't. You can fuck whoever you want. I just didn't want to watch and there wasn't anyone in that bar I wanted to see. If you hurry, you can probably catch him. Don't let me ruin your night."

"Looks like we're interrupting a lover's spat, Billy."

Tristan and Maddox turned and faced the two newcomers. "Can we help you?" Tristan demanded, as he scowled at the two men. "This is a private conversation."

Maddox crossed his arms. "Aren't you the two guys from the other night?"

"Yeah, you surprised us, but we're prepared this time." The guy, who was obviously Billy, pulled out an expandable baton while the other guy cracked his knuckles.

Tristan and Maddox glanced at each other.

Maddox gave him a cheeky smile. "They're human. We got this." He turned back to the men and let his wings spread behind him.

Well shit, Tristan grumbled as he tried to force

his wings to pop out. "This isn't easy without your brand of encouragement."

"Now is not the time to be asking for an ass smacking." Maddox mumbled.

The two men exchanged confused glances before shrugging and charging at them.

Tristan sighed as he dodged the first man with a laugh as he kicked him in the ass. "Not that I'd want you to do that after you picked up a stranger, anyway." Tristan called out as his wings popped out and he smiled. "Finally."

Maddox wrapped his arms around his attacker and squeezed. The muscles of his arms bulged as the guy screamed. He stepped one leg back and threw the guy against the wall of the motel.

"Nice." Tristan called out as he dodged the punch Billy aimed at him. He grabbed the guy's arm and twisted it behind his back. A popping sound filled the air as the man screamed.

"You're stronger than you were. It doesn't take much effort to break their arms." Maddox explained with a shrug. "You'll learn how to limit your strength to deal with humans."

"Well, shit." Tristan cringed. "Really didn't mean to do that. Sorry, Billy."

Maddox's attacker pushed off the wall and

swung at Maddox. He easily dodged him. The man's momentum sent him flying right onto the hood of Scarlet.

Tristan and Billy froze. "Oh shit," Tristan muttered.

Maddox's fists balled at his side. "Oh, you motherfucker. Now you crossed the line."

"Attacking us wasn't crossing a line?"

Maddox charged at the man. Tristan was in awe of the glow emanating from Maddox's wings.

Maddox pulled back and punched the guy so hard his nose instantly started gushing blood as he fell to the ground unconscious.

Billy whimpered as Tristan tightened his grip on the man's broken arm. "Stop, please. I won't fight you. Don't kill me." He pleaded as he dropped to his knees.

Tristan grimaced. "You got any zip ties in Scarlet? Then we can take them to the Agency to sit for the night. Let them think about what's going to happen and we'll talk to them tomorrow."

Maddox nodded and stepped back away from the guy laying on the ground. "Yeah, I'll grab them."

Tristan watched as Maddox headed to his trunk, "Fuck me, this was not how I saw the night going."

"Me either." Billy agreed between whimpers.

CHAPTER
Sixteen

MADDOX HELD the door to the office open and waited for Tristan. "How'd you sleep last night?"

Tristan shrugged and took a sip of his extra large coffee.

They got to the pod and Vic was waiting for them. "Two of the kids go to the same school. The principal asked if we could make an appearance down there and help reassure the kids."

Maddox wasn't sure who groaned louder, Tristan or him. "Kids... really? Can't you send someone more empathetic?"

"Or at least someone that's not an asshole." Tristan grumbled softly.

Vic shrugged. "I'm sure you two want to take a turn with the two guys you brought in last night, but let's let them stew a bit longer and you can have a go with them when you get back from the school."

Tristan crossed his arms and scowled, "Fine, but I'm not wearing that damn P.I.S. vest. When do they want us there?"

"Nine thirty, they're having an assembly with the whole school." Vic replied absently as he looked over some papers he was just handed.

"Fine, I'll meet you there. I have to make a stop." Tristan announced as he turned and headed back to his office.

"How mysterious," Maddox grumbled. He turned back to Vic. "Are you coming too?"

Vic shook his head violently. "Oh, hell no. You wouldn't catch me dead going to a school."

"Oh sure, it's fine to throw us to the wolves." He pointed across the room at Raelle. "Hey, you have a calming effect. Why don't you come?"

She held her hands up apologetically. "Oh sorry, we're running down a bank robbery suspect. Maybe next time." She ducked out of the room before he could respond.

He glanced toward his office and saw Tristan staring at his computer. He couldn't still be mad about the bar last night, could he? Nothing happened. It's not like they were together. He didn't owe him any allegiance.

He stomped down the hall and out to his car. He was not going to feel bad for having a life. The drive to the school didn't take long. He sat in his car until Tristan pulled in. He wasn't going in there alone. "Ready for this?"

Tristan nodded but didn't say a word as he strode past him into the administration building.

"Really, you're going to be like that?" Maddox grumbled loud enough that Tristan had to have heard him, but the other man didn't acknowledge it if so.

Tristan nodded to the secretary behind the counter. "We're with the Paranormal Investigative Services. This is Senior Agent Maddox Smith and I'm Agent Tristan James. We were sent down to talk to the kids, I believe."

"Yes, of course. I just need some identification and I'll have someone escort you to the assembly."

Tristan handed over his P.I.S. wallet with his badge and ID in it.

Once Tristan was given a name badge, he stepped back and let Maddox go next. As he was sticking his name badge on his shirt, a tall woman came out from a back office.

"Gentlemen, thank you for coming. I'm Mrs. Honeywell, I'm the Principal here." She reached out and shook both of their hands. "The kids were scared after the first disappearance, but for it to happen a second time is devastating. We've brought in counselors, but we thought it would be good for them to see you guys and hear that you are working on finding their friends."

Maddox grimaced. No pressure there. After this long, he doubted most of the kids were going to be recovered. Did he really want to give the kids a bunch of false hope? How could they do this without outright lying to them?

"Do they know we're going to be here today? What expectations have they been given? We don't want to mislead them, but I won't lie to them either. I hope you understand we're in a difficult situation here." Tristan explained as they followed after the principal as she led them through the school.

Maddox was relieved Tristan had the same concerns he did. They probably should have talked through a game plan before coming in, but as long as Tristan was icing him out, that wasn't going to happen.

Tristan stopped in his tracks and gaped as he

looked into one of the classrooms they were passing. "What is that?"

Mrs. Honeywell stopped and opened the door to a large two-story tall room. Platforms ran along the walls at varying heights. "This is where the kids come to learn how to fly in a safe environment. You didn't have one of these in your school growing up?"

"Uh, no ma'am. I went to a human school. Up until last week, I thought I was human. This is all new to me, and if I do say so myself. I'm a bit jealous of these kids. Could I come and sit in on a class? It's gotta be better than trying to learn from Mr. Tight ass over there."

She tsked. "Language Mr. James. There are a lot of impressionable young children here." Tristan rolled his eyes as he heard Maddox laughing quietly next to him. "As to your question, I'm sure when the cases have been resolved you're more than welcome to come see what they learn."

Tristan whooped in excitement and then settled down as he felt the disapproving stare of the principal. "Sorry," He winced as he moved to stand behind Maddox and out of her direct line of sight.

She shut the door and continued down the hall. "The auditorium is just ahead. We've already got everyone inside."

As they approached the double doors the noise grew increasingly louder. She held the door open and let them go in first. As kids saw them, they stopped talking. It only took seconds for the quiet to spread.

They were led on stage where several other adults were already seated. Mrs. Honeywell pointed to the last two chairs. "You can sit there while I get started."

You could hear a pin drop as she stepped up to the podium. "Morning everyone. We know there has been a lot going on lately with the disappearances of Derek Rowland and Aurora Massey. We know you have questions and some fear and we brought in some special friends to talk to you. Now please make sure you show our guests the same respect you give me."

She looked back at them and waved them forward. "This is Agent Tristan James and Senior Agent Maddox Smith."

They walked forward awkwardly.

"He's so big." A small girl in the front row whispered loudly.

Tristan grinned down at the small child, "But he's just like a big teddy bear. All cuddly and soft, you don't have to be afraid of him."

Maddox growled as he glared at Tristan, then stepped up to the microphone. "My partner and I work for the Paranormal Investigative Services. We've been working hard on your friend's cases and we're doing everything we can to find the people responsible." He glanced at Tristan and shrugged. What the hell did he say now? "If you have any questions, we'll be happy to answer them."

A boy a few rows back stood up. "Were they taken because they were bad?"

Tristan frowned and stepped forward. "Not at all. Nothing they did caused any of this to happen. The people responsible are bad, not the kids."

A girl in the very back stood up. "Do you think you'll have them back here soon?" Maddox turned wide eyes toward Tristan. Now what the fuck did they say?

"We're going to do everything in our power to bring them home as quickly as we can."

"Well, my dad says that you guys are wasting time and money and that they are probably already dead because you guys are too slow." A girl called out from the middle of the room.

"Jesus Christ." Mrs. Honeywell muttered.

Tristan and Maddox turned, shocked that she cursed after reprimanding Tristan for it. She stepped to the microphone. "Mandy, that is not an appropriate question. We can discuss that one on one after the assembly. Now, who else has a question?"

Hands shot in the air from all over the room.

"This is going to be the longest day of my fucking life." Maddox sighed as he stepped back up to the microphone and pointed to a boy to his right. "Okay, let's hear it." He probably sounded a little too gruff, but that last question really threw him for a loop.

"I heard that Derek's finger was left on his bed for his parents to find. Is that true?"

Maddox threw his head back and stared at the ceiling. "Fuck my life."

Maddox stopped for coffee on his way back to the station. He was tempted to add alcohol, but Vic would probably frown at the idea.

He found Tristan at his desk, studying the files again. "Brought you a coffee, thought you could use it."

Tristan ignored the gesture and kept staring at the files.

"How about this? Let's go take our feelings out on those shitbags from last night?"

"Fine." Tristan growled as he pushed to his feet, leaving the coffee on his desk as he stormed out of the office.

"Fucking child." Maddox rolled his eyes as he followed behind him. He was not going to give him the satisfaction of an apology when he hadn't done anything wrong.

They were quiet as they made their way to the holding cells. As soon as the perps saw them, they rushed to the bars and started yelling at the same time.

"We've been in here for fourteen hours."

"I need food. You can't starve us."

Tristan smiled as he leaned against the bars, "Hey Billy, how's that arm of yours doing?"

"Fuck you man. It hurts, I need something for the pain too. Don't we have rights or something?"

"Rights?" Tristan laughed. "You attacked two federal agents. You gave up your rights. But if you want to come with us and talk, we can re-evaluate after."

"I ain't saying shit." The other asshole argued. "We get one phone call. I want to call my lawyer."

Tristan smirked as he glanced at Maddox, "That's too bad our phones went down, isn't it?"

Maddox went back into the hall and asked for

the key. He came back holding it up. "You're up first, Billy boy."

Unlucky for them, he didn't even put up a fight as he let them lead him to an interrogation room. If he was going to get any of this pent up energy out, he was going to need them to get angry.

They shoved him into a chair and sat across the table from him. Maddox leaned back and glanced at Tristan. "They came after you. Would you like the honors?"

Tristan nodded as he leaned forward and braced his arms on the table. "Billy, why don't you start with telling us your name and why you've been looking for me? Because I know you have, I have witnesses that state you've come by my room multiple times. Why is that?"

Billy pursed his lips as he stared back at them. "I got nothing to say."

Maddox sighed. "You know we're paranormal, right? We have an entire building of scary-ass creatures in here and no one knows we have you. How do you want this to happen?"

"You can't do that, you can't touch me. You're agents and have to protect people. Not hurt them. I want my lawyer."

"Fine," Tristan said as he climbed to his feet.

"Give us a few minutes." He moved to the door and stuck his head out. "Can someone ask Logan to come sit with our friend here, please."

Maddox laughed and then covered it with a cough as he moved to stand beside Tristan. "Logan will sit with you for your safety, of course. Until your lawyer arrives."

They ignored his protests as they shut the door behind them and went to get the next guy.

The guy was sweating as he stared at them through the bars. "I heard Billy yelling, what's going on? What happened to him?"

Maddox shrugged. "I didn't hear anything. These old buildings make some weird noises. Why don't we go have a chat?"

Tristan opened the cell and grabbed the guy by his arm. They led him down the hall. They paused at the room Billy was in and laughed when they looked inside. Logan, in all his Bear glory, was standing over Billy, snarling as drool dripped down his fangs.

They kept going and put him in the next room.

Maddox leaned his hands on the table. "Let's make this easy. You give us your name and why you were stalking my partner here and this will all go away quickly. You know we're going to find out anyway when we process you, so you might as well speak up now and show us you want to be cooperative."

The man sat back and laughed. "Are you pissy because I interrupted something the other night? Does your boss know you were fucking your partner until he passed out and then left?"

Tristan laughed and crossed his arms. "That's funny as shit, man." Tristan winked at the man and then looked up at Maddox. "Maybe he's jealous and wants a piece of you, too. Maybe if he talks, we can release him and you can pick him up later to say thank you for talking."

"What the fuck." The guy growled, "I ain't into no gay bullshit."

Maddox didn't know who he wanted to strangle first, the homophobe across the table or his partner for insinuating he was a slut. He took a deep breath to try to regain his composure. "I don't know. You guys came to his room pretty late the other night. Maybe you were hoping for something else?"

"Fuck no. We were sent there to get him, not fuck him." He raged as spit flew from his mouth with every word.

Tristan laughed as he cocked one eyebrow at the guy. "Who sent you, and why do they want me?

You've already admitted that much. Make it easy on yourself and tell us what we need to know."

Maddox held his breath, thinking the guy was going to give in. Instead, he leaned forward and spit at them. "I'm no narq, go fuck each other."

Tristan glanced up at Maddox. "Do we have any soul eaters here today? Maybe they'd like some time alone with him."

It took Maddox a second to catch up. "Yeah, I think we do. Let's go get him."

They laughed as they walked out to the man raging at them.

In the hall, Maddox stopped Tristan. "What the hell is a soul eater?"

Tristan shrugged, "Fuck if I know, but it sounded scary as shit and it terrified him. So, it was a win-win. Besides, they aren't going to give us shit. They're hired muscles, not the brains."

Maddox nodded in agreement. His cell phone vibrated in his pocket. He glanced at it and saw it was his mom. "Hey mom, what's going on?"

"Oh good, you answered. I'm outside your office. I said I wanted lunch one day and I'm here, so tell Vic you have an errand to run and get out here."

Maddox was torn, but he couldn't leave his mom

hanging, and they were stuck until the goons were processed. "Okay, I'll be right out."

He slid his phone back into his pocket. He glanced at Tristan. "Want to come to lunch with me and my mom?"

Tristan scoffed, "Yeah, I don't think that's a good idea right now. As much as I'd love to meet her, I'm in a shitty ass mood, and I'd make a terrible first impression. And I don't want to insult her son to her face and if I go, I can't guarantee I won't say something."

Maddox's jaw clenched as he stared at him. "You are being such a child. Fine, go do your own thing. Call me when the records are in."

He didn't wait for an answer. He stormed down the hall and outside.

His mom was leaning next to Scarlet, smiling at him. "There's my boy. Vic give you any trouble?"

Maddox shrugged. "I didn't even ask him. I'm starving. Let's get some food."

She kissed his cheek, then climbed into his passenger seat. "Let's go to the Acropolis Greek Tavern. You know I love it there."

"Whatever you want, my treat."

They drove the short distance to the restaurant and got a table.

"So mom, why are you here? Middle of the week visits are unusual for you."

She sipped her water. "Vic mentioned you had a new partner that's a new paranormal and I wanted to check in and see how you were handling it."

Of course, Vic told her. He really hated that his mom and his boss were friends from high school. "His name is Tristan. He was human then got attacked and now he's a stubborn, irritating Phoenix that gets on my last nerve."

He let out a breath when he finished and saw the surprise on her face. "I'm sorry. There's just a lot going on right now and we had a hell of a morning at an elementary school. Tristan is a perfectly acceptable partner."

She quirked an eyebrow at him. "Perfectly acceptable. Your tone implies otherwise."

"Oh for fuck's sake." His mom spun around to see what he was looking at.

"Do you know that man?"

He huffed. "Yep, that would be my new partner. Of course, he would end up at the same restaurant as us."

"Why don't we invite him to join us?"

Maddox shook his head. "No, let's not bother him."

"Nonsense." She got up and rushed to Tristan, who was backing away from the wild-looking stranger coming at him.

Maddox watched them talk. They both glanced at him several times, then Tristan nodded and followed her back to the table.

"Maddox, he said you didn't even invite him to join us."

Maddox glared at Tristan. How dare he lie to his mom. "Yeah sorry, guess I just didn't think about it." He couldn't resist kicking his partner under the table.

Tristan's smirk turned into a scowl as he leaned down and rubbed his leg. "I'm glad I ran into you, Ms. Smith. It's wonderful to meet the woman who is responsible for the man he's become today."

Who the hell is this guy? Laying it on pretty thick.

She chuckled. "How sweet of you, but it's Ms. Traakurk, but you can call me Marta."

"Oh, I'm sorry. I didn't realize you had different last names. Maddox's a bit private on his life, so I only know the basics."

"And he'll tell you I'm a serious oversharer. Maddox changed his last name before going to the academy."

"Mom," Maddox growled. With the weirdness between him and Tristan right now, he didn't really want his family's dirty laundry aired.

She swatted at him. "Oh, stop. He's your partner." She turned back to Tristan. "We have a very traditional last name in the ogre community and when he found out about his dad, he offered him his Fae last name. Mr. Self-Isolated over here decided to shun both names and go with a generic one."

Maddox couldn't stay quiet. "Self-isolating? The ogre's made fun of me for having faery wings and the Fae looked at me like I was grotesque."

She tsked as she leaned toward Tristan. "There has been some ribbing, but he truly does have friends back home who miss him. And his father still asks me often to convince him to visit him in the Fae realm, but you can guess how that goes over."

Tristan nodded sagely, "I've seen that behavior myself. He has this terrible idea that he doesn't deserve anything good. I wondered where it came from."

"You know I'm sitting right here, don't you?" Maddox fumed.

"The truth hurts, but you need to hear it son. You have people who love you, but you keep us at arm's length."

Tristan snorted, "Always avoiding anything meaningful. I've seen that pattern with him already myself."

"I have friends who accept me just the way I am." Maddox crossed his arms.

"Underage prostitutes don't really count, Maddox." Tristan fired back and then winced as he turned to face Marta. "Shit, that came out so wrong. He's friended this teenager named Tallie, and he's been trying to get her into a shelter and off the streets"

Marta clutched her chest. "My soft-hearted boy. You were always so kind."

Maddox wanted to die. This couldn't get any more mortifying.

Thankfully, he didn't have to respond. The food came and distracted them from talking about him any longer. Putting his mom and Tristan in the same room together was definitely not a good idea.

CHAPTER
Seventeen

TRISTAN DROPPED into the seat of his truck with a sigh. Lunch had been delicious, but frustrating. He was glad he'd had the chance to meet Marta and get a bit of background on Maddox and what made him tick. He'd tried really hard to keep the snark and jibes under control, but he'd failed a few times. Luckily, Maddox's mother didn't seem to catch them. The last thing he wanted was for her to dislike him.

He frowned as he drove back to the station as his head circled that thought. Why did he care so much if she liked him? It wasn't like he was likely to spend much time with her in the future. For that matter, why was he still so bitter over Maddox almost going home with some twink from the bar? They weren't in a relationship and weren't likely to ever start one, even if he was attracted to the asshole. Relationships didn't work between work partners, too much time spent together and one side or the other would grow to resent the other.

As he walked into their pod, Cross called out the files they'd been waiting for were ready on his desk. Tristan waved a thank you and sat at his desk to review the information on the would-be assassins.

Both men had extensive rap sheets going back to their juvenile years. Mostly petty crimes and assault. They'd both done a few years of time, but nothing recently. Hell, their records for the last couple of years were clean, too. He frowned and sat back in his chair. No way in hell they'd gone clean, so how had they made it that long without getting busted?

Maddox walked in and plopped down in his chair. He stared at his screen as he mumbled to Tristan. "Thanks for being nice to my mom. I appreciate it."

Tristan grunted as he spun in his chair, lost in his thoughts. He sat up, grabbed the files, and tossed them to Maddox's desk. "See anything odd there?"

Maddox flipped through the pages, going back and forth between the files. "How did these two go from constant trouble to model citizens?"

"Exactly. Things aren't adding up here at all." Tristan grumbled as he leaned his head back against the headrest and stared at the ceiling. "And they went from petty crimes to attempted murder. That's quite a big jump, if you ask me. I feel like I'm missing something, but I can't figure it out. It's right there, just out of my grasp."

"Were they ever in the same jail at the same time? I'm trying to figure out how these two got connected." Maddox asked as he tossed a rubber band ball in the air and caught it.

Tristan shrugged. "Didn't get that far yet, to be honest. This place has all kinds of high-tech shit, don't we have something that can scan both files and spit out any connections? It'd make our jobs a shit ton easier."

Maddox pushed out of his chair. "We don't but Cole is our techno nerd for this team. I bet he can whip something up for us."

"Good idea." Tristan jumped up, grabbed both files, and headed out into the pod, calling Cole's name.

Cole stuck his head out of his door and frowned. "What are you hollering about? I'm right here. You don't have to scream."

Tristan shrugged, "I didn't know which office was

yours and this was quicker." He said as he stepped around the Koala shifter and dropped the files on his desk. "I'm told you're the man to see about writing an algorithm that can find similarities between these two files quickly."

Cole shrugged. "Sure, that's easy. How quick do you need it? I'm kind of busy."

"As soon as you can, I'll take you to dinner as a thank you."

"Sure, sounds good." Cole shooed Tristan out of the room. "Let me get to work and we can talk food later."

Tristan laughed as he left his office. "It's a date."

Maddox was leaning against their office doorjamb with his arms crossed. He didn't say a word as Tristan walked back inside.

He chuckled as he sat in his chair and pulled a file up on his computer. He hadn't spent much time with Cole, but the guy had a good sense of humor and seemed like he'd be somebody he could be friends with. Maybe dinner would be the beginning of a new bestie in his life. He halfheartedly watched from the corner of his eye as Maddox frowned at him and moved back to his desk. Why was he frowning at him now? Damn man, made no sense most of the time.

"Hey have we heard anything about the human files?" Tristan asked absently as he pretended to study the blank screen on his computer.

"No luck last I heard."

"Alright, I'm stepping in and contacting someone on the force who I think will help us. Will you let Vic know, and I'll call my friend now?"

Tristan didn't wait for Maddox to reply, just pulled his phone out and searched his contacts for the rookie's name. He'd never actually talked to the kid before he helped him move his shit. But they'd all traded numbers in case they'd needed to reach someone, and for once he was glad they had.

The phone rang three times before he heard a hesitant hello come across the line. "Jaylen, this is Tristan James." The silence stretched for a few moments until Tristan was tempted to pull the phone away to make sure the call hadn't been dropped.

"Uh, yeah, hey. Give me a second to get some-place I can talk."

Tristan drummed his fingers on the desk as he waited for what seemed like an eternity before the kid came back on the phone. "Hey Tristan, what's up?"

"I know this is out of the blue and you can say

no, but I need a favor and I don't know who else I can talk to. Can you meet me for a drink and I'll explain?"

"Yeah, I think so. Where and when?"

Tristan hesitated as he glanced up at Maddox. "You comfortable going to Tanners?"

"Never been there, but I've heard of it. If they'll let me in I have no problem going there." Jaylen answered without hesitation.

"Yeah, shouldn't be an issue. Can you meet me in like an hour?"

"Yeah, I'm coming." Jaylen called out, "Listen man. I gotta go, but I'll see you in an hour."

"See you then." He replied as he heard the phone click. "He's in. We should have the files hopefully by tomorrow afternoon, if he agrees to help."

Tristan pushed his chair back and grabbed his things. "I'm going to head over there and be ready when he shows up just in case he comes early. If you want to join us, you're welcome." Tristan wasn't sure why he said that. Part of him was still mad. But he couldn't not give Maddox the chance to be involved in anything pertaining to the cases. He'd just have to make sure he kept things professional when they were alone.

Maddox walked over to his computer and logged

out of it. "Sure, I'll tag along. I don't spend much time with humans that aren't criminals, so this'll be a nice change of pace."

"Sounds good. I'll meet you there." Tristan called out as he headed out of their office without waiting for Maddox.

It only took him a few minutes to get to the bar at this time of the day. He grabbed a prime spot and climbed out. He waved hello to Froggy and took in the empty room. He moved to an empty booth in the back corner and sat down with a sigh.

"You want a drink? Or are you just going to hide and sulk in the corner?" Froggy hollered across the empty bar.

"As long as it isn't one of those damn things you gave me the other night, I'll happily take a drink. One that won't knock me on my ass this time, maybe?"

Froggy laughed, "No promises. I didn't expect you to be such a lightweight after all."

Maddox walked in and right up to the bar, "Hey give me whatever you have on tap."

Tristan watched as Froggy gave Maddox two pints of beer. Maddox laughed at something he said as he walked over to the booth and set the cups down. "This okay?"

"Sure." Tristan shrugged as he took a sip of the dark amber liquid. "Shit, that's really good."

Maddox nodded as he took a large gulp.

After a few minutes of silence, Maddox slammed his cup down. "Fine, let's have it out. You want me to apologize for being lonely and going out with someone? I don't think that's very fair of you."

Tristan cocked one eyebrow. "Did I ask you to apologize for that?"

"It sure as shit seems so. You've been a moody bitch since it happened." Maddox accused.

Tristan chewed his lip for a minute as he studied his beer and shrugged. "It's fucking irrational, I know, but I can't help it. You made it worse though asshole. Why did you have to chase after me? You should have just gone home with the guy. But no, you had to come barreling after me and start shit."

"Because somehow, in the short amount of time I've known you, I've come to care about you and what you think of me. Fuck knows why. I saw the look on your face when you saw us and it gutted me. I had to go after you." Maddox blew out a breath as he leaned back against the booth.

"What the fuck is wrong with me? I've never acted like that before. I just saw you touching him, getting ready to get in Scarlet with him and I got so pissed and hurt and I had to get out of there before I saw anything more. I've known you a couple of days. This doesn't make any fucking sense, but now every time I look at you, all I can see is that asshole in your arms, and it makes my blood boil."

Maddox opened his mouth to respond, but stopped when the door opened.

Jaylen, in plain clothes, walked in, looking around nervously. Tristan waved at him. "Over here."

Jaylen rushed across the bar. Tristan got up and sat on the same side as Maddox to give him more room.

"Hey man, thanks for coming. This is my partner, Maddox. Maddox, this is Jaylen, he's a rookie on the TPD." Tristan introduced the two men and waved to Froggy to bring another drink over.

"Thanks," Jaylen said as a beer was set in front of him. "It's nice to meet you, Maddox. And Tristan, you're looking like you healed up nice. It's good to see you back on your feet."

"I don't know if I ever thanked you for your help that day, but thanks." Tristan offered with a sheepish smile. "I was a bit of a mess, as you can imagine."

Jaylen nodded. "It's all good. I didn't need a thanks for being a decent human being. If it helps, your old partner is a mess. He's not been handling shit well at all. He blames himself for not being there and you getting attacked."

Tristan scoffed, "That's bullshit. If he'd been there, he'd probably be dead. I'm glad he wasn't. He may have turned his back on me, but that doesn't mean I wish that on him."

"So, what did you need help with? Not that I mind meeting you for drinks, of course." Jaylen grinned and then shrugged. "If I can do it, I will. Just ask."

"You know those missing kid's cases I was working on before I got kicked off the force, well I think they're related in some way to a rash of missing paranormal kids. I want to compare the files and was wondering if there's any chance you can get your hands on a copy of them."

Jaylen frowned. "Shit, I didn't know both sides had kids disappearing. Yeah, I'll figure it out and get you a copy. Politics be damned, innocent kids don't deserve to be in the crossfire."

Tristan let out a relieved breath and offered his hand to Jaylen, "I'll owe you big time for this and if you get any flack, let us know and we'll see if our ASAC can step in."

Maddox held his hand out. Jaylen glanced at it

and hesitated for a second before grabbing it and shaking it.

They waited until he was gone before relaxing.

Maddox chuckled. "I think he was waiting to see if my hand was going to transform and bite him or something."

"Nah, he's got family that's paranormal. He was probably more worried that you'd crush his hand or something. Did you see how yours engulfed his? He's tiny compared to you."

"If you think my hands are big..." he trailed off and finished his beer in one long gulp.

Froggy burst into laughter as Tristan gaped at Maddox. He turned and glared at Froggy. "You could at least pretend not to listen in on people's private conversations."

Froggy shrugged. "I need some form of entertainment, and watching you two stumble around each other has been the highlight of my week."

"Fucking paranormals," he grumbled as he walked out with a laugh, completely forgetting that he himself was one now too.

CHAPTER
Eighteen

MADDOX GULPED down the last of his drink and tossed money on the table. His cell phone vibrated in his pocket.

The screen showed an unknown number. "This is Agent Smith."

"Maddox, I need you."

His heart sped up. "Tallie, what's wrong? Where are you?"

The fear in the girl's voice was palpable. "I was being chased by some guys. I ran into a building and I'm hiding. I'm afraid to leave."

Maddox took long strides out the door hoping to catch Tristan before he pulled out. "What building, I'll come get you?"

She panted rapidly on the phone. "I don't know. I

was on Kennedy and Ashley and turned onto a bunch of small streets and ran through a park."

Maddox ran toward Tristan's truck and waved his arm to stop him. "Good Tallie, can you see any other buildings or signs from where you're hiding now?"

"Let me move to the window. One minute. I can see that pointy building that always lights up for events and I can hear Jamaican music."

"Okay. Stay quiet and call me back if you need me. We'll be there soon." He hung up and stopped next to Tristan's window. "I need your help. Tallie is in trouble and doesn't know exactly where she's at. Will you help me search?"

"Of course. Do you have any ideas where to start?"

Nausea was overwhelming him. "She said she was on Kennedy and Ashley and from her hiding spot, she can see the old SunTrust Tower, the one that's Truist Place now. Oh, and she hears Jamaican music."

"SunTrust Tower and Jamaican music." Tristan repeated, and then nodded. "I know of one place that fits that. It's on East Twigg street and North Florida Avenue. Let's split up and meet at that corner."

"I'll start on Florida." Maddox waited for Tristan

to nod, then he ran for Scarlet. Thankfully, they were close enough they could get there in less than ten minutes.

They sped through the streets with their lights and sirens blaring. He skidded to a stop at Kennedy and Florida and left his lights flashing as he took off on foot. He grabbed his phone and dialed Tallie's number back. "Did you hear the sirens? That's us. We're here. Just stay put. We're coming for you."

"Thank you, Maddox, please hurry."

He hung up and called Tristan. "Anything yet?"

"No, but there aren't many places she could have gone to hide that fit the descriptions she gave us. I don't see anybody acting weird besides us, either."

"Agreed. I'm already one block down and haven't found an empty building yet. I'll call you if I find something." He hung up and jogged further down until he found an abandoned building. With his gun drawn, he went floor by floor. Other than a few homeless people, there was no sign of Tallie.

He left and kept running. The Jamaican music got louder as he got closer to the restaurant. He skidded to a stop in front of another empty building at the same time Tristan turned the corner and stopped. "Let's hope it's this one."

Tristan nodded as he glanced around, "It fit's

what we're looking for and I noticed a for sale sign on the other side of the building."

Maddox pulled the wood panel covering the broken door aside and climbed in. He pointed at Tristan to go left while he took the right. They went floor by floor until they hit the fourth floor.

Maddox growled as he put his gun away. "Damn it, where the hell is she?"

"Call her and see if we can hear the ring of the phone or her voice. We've got enhanced hearing, right? We should be able to track her even if she whispers."

Maddox steadied his breathing and dialed the number. After two rings, Tristan held up a finger and cocked his head. He waved at Maddox to follow him. They took the stairs back down a floor and heard her whispered hello. "Tallie, it's us. Can you peek your head out and look for us?"

Maddox walked toward the center of the empty area and turned in a circle until he heard her breathing coming from a back corner. They ran over and pushed empty boxes out of the way and found her balled up in a broken part of the wall. "We got you, come on."

They each held out a hand and pulled her up.

She collapsed into Maddox's arms, sobbing. "It's okay, we got you."

"Let's get her out of here." Tristan murmured from beside them. "Tallie, are you hurt? Do you need a doctor?"

She shook her head against his shoulder. "No, other than some scratches from falling a couple of times, I'm fine. Don't make me go to a shelter tonight, please."

Maddox's eyes bulged as he glanced over at Tristan. "You don't have to go anywhere you don't want to."

They stayed quiet as he carried her back to his car and put her in the passenger seat. He closed the door and leaned against the hood. "What the hell am I going to do with her? I don't think it's appropriate for me to bring a minor back to my condo."

"We can see if there is a room available close to mine?" Tristan offered with a shrug.

"I have a feeling she isn't going to want to be alone." He bit his lip as he wracked his brain for what to do. "What if you stayed at my place, too?"

Tristan licked his lips and glanced away nervously. "How exactly would that work? You've got a spare room or two?"

"I have a king-sized bed and a pullout couch. I would give her the bedroom so she could have a locked door to feel safe and we could take the couch? Or I could sleep on the floor and you can have the pullout?"

"My motel has two double beds, but that probably wouldn't be smart either." Tristan hesitated. "Shit, I don't think we have a choice. But the thought of making you sleep on the floor in your own place doesn't sit right with me."

"How about we flip for it when we get there? In the meantime, you stop at your place and grab some clothes. I'll order pizza along the way so we can have dinner when we get there."

"Yeah, but if you put pineapple on my pizza, we're going to have a major issue, and you will automatically get the floor."

Maddox held his hands up defensively. "I'm not a psychopath. I believe no veggies should ever be put on pizza. But I always keep fresh pineapple around, you know, because of the added benefit of making me taste good, too."

Tristan blushed as he shook his head and ignored that last part. "Tomatoes are veggies, you know, so you lost that argument already."

Maddox chuckled at Tristan's obvious evasion of his pineapple remark. "The tomato is turned into a sauce, so it's no longer a veggie. I'll die on this hill, so save your breath. Now get your shit and I'll text you my address."

Maddox slid into the driver's seat and checked on Tallie. She was asleep against the door. Adrenaline will do that to you. Now he had to make it through the night with letting people stay over. When he did bring guys back to his place, it was always for a couple of hours of pleasure, then he sent them on their way. He hated the next morning awkwardness. Now he'll have a teenage girl and his partner there. He was an adult, he could do this.

CHAPTER
Nineteen

TRISTAN GROANED as he sat up on the edge of the pull-out bed, "Fucking hell, the floor might have been more comfortable than this piece of shit."

Maddox laughed as he sat up. "I've never slept on it. I had no idea how bad it was. I'm burning this couch and buying a new one."

"Morning." Tallie greeted as she opened the bedroom door tentatively and stepped out with a shy smile.

Tristan grabbed the sheet on the bed and pulled it over his bare legs with a sheepish smile. "How you feeling this morning?"

Tallie laughed, "You don't have to be shy. I've seen bare legs before."

Maddox grabbed the pillow and stood up with it in front of his groin. "It's not about being embarrassed, it's about being appropriate in front of you. If it's okay with you guys, I'll shower and change really quick." He scurried out of the room, leaving Tristan alone with her.

Tristan shot Maddox a glare and then smiled at the teen, "So, uh, I bet we can find some coffee and maybe something to cook for breakfast if you're hungry."

"Sure, I'll see what I can find while you get dressed. He's only got the one bathroom though, so you'll have to share or change in the bedroom with him." She winked as she turned and headed into the small kitchen.

Tristan dropped his head back and let out a low groan. Now he had images of Maddox climbing out of the shower in all his naked glory with water dripping down his body. How was he supposed to get dressed when he was hard as a fucking rock?

He climbed to his feet, grabbed his bag and raced into the bedroom as quickly as he could so Tallie wouldn't see him. He slammed the door shut and leaned against it with a relieved sigh. Thirty-six years old and he was hiding his erection like a teenage boy. He used to have better control over himself.

He took in the room that belonged to his enigma of a partner and frowned. It was sparse and almost barren, with very little personal effects. He dropped his bag on the bed and started rifling through it as he continued to look around. Just as he pulled his boxers off, he heard the bathroom door behind him click open.

"Um, if you wanted to shower with me, you could have just asked." Maddox leaned against the doorjamb with his arms crossed across the chest and nothing on, not even a towel.

"Just that easy, huh?" Tristan scowled at him over his shoulder. "I should have come in and said Maddox, let's save water and you'd have let me climb in there with you? No questions asked?"

"I can be a gentleman. Are you saying you couldn't keep your hands off me? It would be too enticing for you?"

Tristan turned until he was facing Maddox and put his hands on his hips in annoyance, not even caring that he was saluting the other man. "My hands maybe, but no promises on anything else. But don't worry, I'm not going to beg you for anything. No matter if your little friend is up for the task."

Maddox gasped. "Little? Dude, you must be blind. I'm not egotistical, but I can definitely say I'm well hung and proud of it."

Tristan huffed, grabbed his clothes, and pushed past Maddox. "My turn in the shower." He grumbled. He dropped his clothes on the bathroom counter and leaned his head against the wall as he tried to get himself under control. His body was warring with itself. His mind said danger and his cock said come to daddy. His heart, on the other hand, was screaming caution. Three very different emotions battling for dominance, and his resolve was weakening. The only thing that kept him from throwing himself at his partner was how flippant he was in regards to sex.

With a sigh, he jumped in the shower and let the hot water drain away most of his worries, all except the one between his legs that continued to throb. He glanced into the bathroom and listened to the sounds he could hear through the cracked door. When he was sure he was alone, he sighed and gave in to temptation.

Tristan entered the kitchen to find Maddox sitting on one of the bar stools facing the kitchen as Tallie worked at the stove with a smile.

"Good timing," Tallie called out, "I'm just about done."

Maddox sipped his orange juice and ignored Tristan as he sat next to him. Tallie set plates down in front of them with eggs and bacon. After a few bites, Maddox pointed at Tallie. "We talked, and she's going to hang here today while I'm at work and then I'll try to find her a place for tonight. Hopefully, we won't need to displace you for a second night."

"Sounds good." Tristan said between bites, "This is really good."

Tallie beamed, "It's not much, but thanks." She moved closer to the counter and leaned against it. "Thank you both for coming for me last night. I know I'm not your problem, but you didn't even hesitate. I promise I'll try to stay out of your way and not be a pest."

"We just want you safe, kid." Tristan took a sip of his coffee and groaned. "So good. Anyway, I can handle staying here a few days if that's what it takes to make sure you've got someplace to go that works for you and that we trust."

Tristan finished the last bite on his plate and leaned back with a pat to his stomach. "Just don't keep cooking like this or I'll gain too much weight and get fired again."

Tallie laughed as she took his plate and put it in the sink. "I'll take care of the dishes. You guys go to work."

Maddox pushed in his chair and stretched. "I know how I left everything, don't go snooping through my stuff." He ruffled her hair, then grabbed his keys and made his way to the door.

Tristan grinned and winked at Tallie. "We can do it later together and see if we can find some good blackmail." He grabbed his keys and headed out the door to Tallie's laughter.

He jogged up to his truck and climbed into the seat. Out of the corner of his eye, he saw Maddox climbing into Scarlet. He waited until he'd pulled out of the lot before he followed after him. Within a few minutes, they were parking side by side and heading inside.

"The results of the comparison came in." Cole called as soon as they entered the pod. "I put them on your desk, Tristan."

"Thanks, man." Tristan waved as he beelined it

into his office to grab the paper. He scowled as he noticed how short the list was. "Are you fucking kidding me," He growled as he slapped the paper back down on the desk.

Maddox scowled as he moved to grab the paper. "They were both arrested by James Bouchard multiple times, that's their only connection." Maddox turned to Tristan and cocked an eyebrow. "That name mean anything to you?"

Tristan nodded as he began to pace the confines of their office. "Yeah, he now goes by Chief Bouchard."

"Could be a coincidence." Maddox offered absently as he studied the paper clutched in his hands.

"Yeah, maybe," Tristan mumbled softly. "Are we sure there isn't anything else that connects them and we just missed it? Do you know how many people I've arrested since I joined the force? And the Chief has been doing this a lot longer than me."

"That's valid." Maddox agreed as he dropped the paper and turned to face Tristan again, "We can try and talk to them again, see if they've decided to open up a bit more after their scare. Maybe it jogged a memory or something."

"I guess." He agreed half-heartedly. In his heart, he knew that they'd already given up all that they were going to give. They either didn't know anything or were too afraid to tell them anything else.

He was lost in thought when the ringing of his phone startled him. "Agent James speaking."

"This is Dr. Obinski from Shifter General. My staff has been trying to reach you about a checkup, and have been unsuccessful. I pulled some strings and got this number. I hope that's okay."

"Oh yeah, hey." Tristan replied cautiously. "That's fine, I don't mind."

"I'd like you to come in and see me tomorrow as a follow up. I'm not expecting any issues, but you're the first patient I've had contact with who has..." He trailed off and let out a small laugh. "I can't think of the proper word to use in this situation."

Tristan frowned. "So, this is a routine checkup? The hospital didn't tell me I should follow up with you or anyone, to be honest."

"I know." Dr Obinski agreed readily. "I looked over your discharge papers. I'm not sure if you're aware, but seeing your human doctor isn't going to be enough now that you're paranormal. I'm not saying you need to switch to me, but until you find someone and since I was there and know what happened; I'd like to do a checkup and make sure you're aware of some of the changes you'll face now, medically at least."

"Okay, what's your address and what time should I be there, Doc?" Tristan asked as he grabbed a pen and piece of paper. As soon as he hung up, he leaned back in his chair, lost in thought.

"What was that about?" Maddox questioned. "Why do you need to see a doctor?"

Tristan shrugged. "Just wants to check in and fill me in on some things he said." He sighed as he leaned forward and grabbed the paper Maddox had set back down. "Maybe it's time we call the Chief and see if he has any answers on my case. The last time I asked, things devolved quickly, and I didn't get anywhere. It's been a week. They should have come up with something and while we're there, we can ask him about these two and see what happens."

"Sounds good." Maddox agreed as he studied Tristan. "Do we need to talk about what happened this morning, or are we okay?"

Tristan laughed, "I think every time we talk, one of us ends up pissed off. Let's just stop and ignore it all. I don't think it's worth fighting at this point."

After an awkward and silent ride, Tristan pulled into a visitor spot at the Tampa Police Department parking lot and scowled as he took it all in. He'd spent countless hours in this building and now, because of one freak twist of fate, he wasn't welcome. It was a bitter pill to swallow on the best of days, and today was not one of those.

"We going in?"

"Last time he made me wait for hours, you ready for that if he does it again?" Tristan asked as he grabbed the folder with the information on their two assailants.

"I wouldn't miss the opportunity to sit there and make them all uncomfortable." Maddox smiled ruefully.

Tristan nodded and grabbed his phone. "Let me text Jaylen and see if we can kill two birds with one stone while we're here. He might not be comfortable meeting us, but it won't hurt to see how he feels about it."

Before he had time to put his phone away, Jaylen had already texted back. "He says he'll meet us when the meeting is over. He'll be around all day."

"Brave kid, too bad he's not a supe. We could use

him." Maddox said as he followed Tristan toward the entrance.

Tristan scoffed, "maybe it's time the powers that be wake up and make a joint agency made up of humans and paranormals. We'll never get past the hatred if we can't show a united front."

Maddox chuckled, "Hatred is definitely taught."

"I think both sides blame the other for the realm fusion and the changes it caused." Tristan shrugged. "Not to mention our government requiring the genetic testing and cataloging of paranormals. You know I'd never thought about it till now, but that's some bullshit."

"The reason why we are tested is bullshit, but humans are getting tested too, so at least it's happening to both sides."

"Wait," Tristan gaped as he turned to face Maddox, "That's right, we're all tested at birth, so wouldn't it have been known that I have the paranormal gene too?"

Maddox cocked his head to the side. "Actually, yeah, you would think so. Maybe your doctor friend can answer that one."

They headed to the elevators, lost in their thoughts. Tristan did his best to ignore the stares and whispered comments. By the time the doors opened and they stepped inside, his blood pressure was through the roof. He blew out a breath and stabbed the button for the Chief's floor.

"Fucking assholes." He mumbled as he leaned against the wall with a scowl.

Maddox patted his shoulder. "Just remember you had the same prejudices as them a week ago, and it's not their fault." He twisted his face. "I just realized you are changing me. I was like them too, but I'm starting to realize our attitudes are the problem."

"We still have our issues with each other, but it's not because of our species at least." Tristan smirked as he walked off the elevator and to the Chiefs receptionist's desk. "We need to see him."

"Do you have an appointment?" She sneered.

Tristan scoffed, "Nope, just tell him who's here and that we'll sit here all day, every day, until he sees us."

"And," Maddox interjected quickly, "We'll bring friends so that your little waiting room is filled with our kind."

"You do realize this is a police station, right? I think we'd outnumber you." She rolled her eyes as she pushed out of her chair and entered the door behind her.

Tristan cocked an eyebrow. "You really thought that would work?"

"No, but I'm having too much fun to care." Maddox grinned.

They moved to the small waiting room and sat down. Tristan tried not to think too hard on the last time he'd been in this position. His life had been falling apart, or at least he'd thought so. It was kind of insane how much had changed in one short week.

"The Chief will see you now." The receptionist announced in her shrewish voice.

Tristan climbed to his feet and smiled at her. "Thank you." He wiped the fake smile from his face as they entered the chief's office and moved to stand in front of the man's desk.

"Mr. James." The chief greeted, "And I'm sorry I didn't get your name."

"Senior Special Agent Smith." Maddox replied as he stopped beside Tristan. "And it's Agent James, now."

Chief Bouchard sighed and leaned back in his chair, "What is it you gentleman want? I'm a busy man and can't spare the time for trivial things today."

"You don't even know what we want. How do you

know it's trivial?" Maddox questioned, then crossed his arms and rolled his eyes when he was ignored.

"First off, I'd like to know what the status of my case is? Has there been any headway? Suspects?" Tristan asked as he dropped into the chair beside him and rested his hands on the armrests, so he appeared relaxed.

"As I told you before, when we have something to report, we'll call you. Coming here bugging me is not going to help. We have officers on the case and they are reporting directly to me because of the sensitive nature of the case."

"Why?" Tristan demanded, "Why to you, unless you suspect another officer to have been involved, this should be standard procedure."

"Nonsense," The Chief scoffed. "There has been a bit of media attention since it was an attack on a member of the force. This is simply to contain the leakage of sensitive information, nothing more. I assume you haven't been bothered by anyone since we are keeping the location of the motel you are staying at quiet."

Maddox nudged Tristan. "Guess we're not the only ones who tracked you illegally."

Tristan studied the chief. He knew the other man was lying but he couldn't quite place his finger on which parts he was being untruthful on. "Speaking of that. The second reason we're here today is in an official capacity. We detained two men for an attempted assault at my motel. They attacked us, and when we looked into their records, the only connection we could find between them was you."

The chief's jaw tightened as he stared them down. It was several seconds of dead silence as they waited to see who would break first. "And what is it exactly you're saying?"

"Nothing," Tristan grinned, "We were just hoping to see if you remember either of the men and if maybe they were connected to the attack on me last week."

"Who are they?" Chief Bouchard asked as he leaned forward and laced his hands together. "I can see if they are on our suspect list or if their names have come up in our investigation." He cocked one eyebrow and smiled. "And to my connection, I doubt there is one. As you know, in the course of our careers, we arrest hundreds of people."

Tristan shrugged, "That's true. I said that as well, but it's interesting that literally the only thing these two men have in common is you."

Maddox flipped open the file and placed one of the pictures on the table before the Chief, "Billy

Masterson." He laid the second one down next to it, "Brick Freeman,".

Chief Bouchard studied both pictures and then glanced back up at them. "I'm sorry I don't recognize either man, and they aren't on our list of suspects at this time."

Tristan frowned as he studied the other man. He was as cool as a cucumber, giving nothing away. But there was something scratching in the back of his mind, saying he was missing something important. The Chief knew more than he was letting on. Tristan was sure of it. He just wasn't sure if it was in regards to their two suspects or his attack at the house.

Maddox held up a finger. "Actually, we have a third topic. We've been trying to reach out to your office to get some case files from you. We have several missing kids and Tristan said you guys do too. We think there might be a connection, but our boss hasn't been able to get any cooperation from your side."

The chief shook his head. "I haven't been told anything about that. I'll check with my assistant and see why we haven't gotten the files to you. I can't imagine they are connected, though."

Maddox stood up. "Well, I guess we better get back to the office and keep interviewing Billy and

Brick. If we put enough pressure on them, they'll give up names. Humans never last long during one of our interrogations."

Tristan followed his partner out of the office as he pulled his phone out of his pocket and texted Jaylen to arrange a meetup to grab the files. As soon as they were back in the elevator he smiled, "He's hiding something, but I just can't put my finger on what."

"If he is involved in all this, he is a master liar. He never flinched or let on that he knew the guys or anything about the files. It was impressive, really."

"Guess that's what fast tracked him up the ranks to Chief. I don't trust the fucker, though." Tristan replied as he checked his phone. "Jaylen said he'll meet us in the bathrooms by the cells." Tristan shuddered as he put his phone away. "They are gross, but always empty. It's a good call. No one will interrupt us there."

"I've had my fair share of secret bathroom meetings, but this is by far going to be the most boring one."

"Why does that not surprise me," Tristan frowned. He waited until the doors opened and he could step out and then said, "Guess I should be lucky you're not into Jaylen, or this could get really awkward fast."

"He's not really my type. I like them with a little more fire." Maddox winked as he walked out.

Tristan gaped in shock as he followed Maddox down the hall. Was that a nod to his phoenix, or was Maddox just playing with him? He wasn't sure how to reply or even if he should. He sighed and called out, "Do you know where you're going?"

"Use your shifter senses. I can hear the cell doors opening and closing so I generally know which direction. I assumed you'd say something if I went the wrong way."

"Maybe." He grumbled softly. When would he learn to use his paranormal abilities and stop thinking of himself as human with limits?

"Stop staring at my ass, Tristan." Maddox laughed as he stopped outside the bathroom doors. "This the right place?"

"You're such an asshole," Tristan grumbled as he pushed past Maddox and entered the bathroom. "You should feel right at home here, I'd say."

"Don't hate the player, hate the game," Maddox shot back.

"Guess if you're admitting you're a player, that's half the battle."

The door swung open behind them. Jaylen peeked in and shuffled past them. "This is probably the dumbest thing a rookie could do, but the kids are more important." He opened his backpack and pulled out a stack of folders. "This is everything I could get my hands on."

"I know man, and we really appreciate you going out on a limb like this. We'll keep your name out of things, and if ever we can bring on humans, you'll be the first we recruit." Tristan took the files and clapped him on the shoulder. "If it helps, this might help us bring these kids home."

"You do that and no matter what, this will have been worth it." Jaylen agreed. "I've got to go before someone gets suspicious."

Tristan nodded and watched as he ran out of the bathroom. "I think he's afraid to be alone with you in here. Maybe your reputation precedes you." Tristan laughed as he left the bathroom and headed back to their car.

Maddox snorted. "If my reputation is known in the human world too, then I'm definitely doing something right." He unlocked Scarlet and slid into the driver's seat. "Do you want me to run you by the motel before we go back to my place?"

"Only if you're giving me a ride in tomorrow. My truck is back at the agency."

"You're a needy partner, you know that." He threw his head back and laughed as he peeled out of the parking lot.

Needy my ass, Tristan grumbled to himself as he grabbed the oh shit bar to keep himself from falling into his partner's lap.

CHAPTER
Twenty

MADDOX PULLED into the spot in front of Tristan's motel room and pulled out his phone. While he waited for the other man to grab stuff, he texted Tallie.

Maddox: We're on our way home. Want Chinese for dinner?"

Tallie: Gee thanks dad, that sounds yummy.

Maddox: I'm not that old! What do you want and we'll order it to be delivered?

Tallie: Garlic chicken with white rice please. Oooh, can you get some of those crunchy noodles too?

Maddox: Geez, two needy people in my life. What did I do to deserve this?

Tallie sent back a gif of a girl blowing him kisses.

For all his grumbling, it was kind of nice having someone to go home to. Not sure what it says that it's a baby supe and a teenage prostitute.

Tristan plopped down into Scarlet's seat and tossed a bag into the back seat. "What's got you smiling like that? You score another hookup?"

"Not everything is about sex hornball. I was talking to Tallie, I'm ordering Chinese." He opened an app on his phone and tossed it to Tristan. "My order is already saved in there. Add whatever you want and garlic chicken with white rice for Tallie. It'll be there by the time we get home."

Tristan laughed. "You're the one who's been making comments about his bathroom escapades. Don't blame me for assuming the worst."

Maddox cranked up the radio. After a few minutes, Tristan tossed the phone back at him. "I paid using the card you had saved in the app. I'll give you some cash."

Maddox shrugged but didn't respond.

They parked in the assigned spot as the delivery

guy pulled up. "Maddox, are you extra hungry tonight? This is way more than your usual order?"

Maddox grabbed the bag from the teenager. "I have guests over, actually."

"Woah, you have friends?" The boy glanced at Tristan and burst out laughing.

Maddox scowled at him. "I think your tip is shrinking."

The teen held his hands up. "Relax man, I'm just giving you shit. See you next week." He waved before speeding off.

"I'm going to guess he's too young for your tastes. So the food must be really good."

Maddox quirked an eyebrow at him. "Hornball." He pushed the lock button on Scarlet and walked away. It was starting to bother him Tristan had such a low opinion of him, but he had no way to change that now. The best he could do was keep teasing him.

"Honey, we're home." He called out as he went inside.

Tallie popped up from the couch. "Thank god. I have been so freaking bored."

Maddox shook his head. "The shelter's more entertaining?"

She shrugged as she dug through the bag of food. "No but at least I wasn't alone."

Maddox knew exactly how she felt. He hated the quiet of the apartment. That was usually when he'd end up at the bar looking for a fling.

"Hopefully all that boredom worked up an appetite, cause this smells amazing." Tristan said as he went into the kitchen and began to open drawers. "Where in the hell is your silverware, man? Nothing is where it should be. What is wrong with you?" He grumbled as he slammed them closed and opened the next.

"You got your way, and I got mine, don't like it, eat with your fingers." He replied as he opened the drawer next to the fridge and grabbed forks.

"Can you guys hurry up? Let's eat and then stream a movie."

They laughed at the whiny tone of her voice. She really didn't handle being on her own that well. How on Earth was she managing the nights she was out on the streets?

They ate quickly while Tallie rambled about everything and nothing. The girl had an endless amount of air.

"Can I do a load of laundry before we start watching the movie? I don't have anything clean to wear to work tomorrow." Tristan asked as he cleaned up his mess from dinner.

Maddox pointed down the hall with his elbow as he walked toward the kitchen. "It's in the closet at the end of the hall. Have at it."

Tristan opened his duffle bag and dug a pile of clothes out of it.

Maddox leaned back to look down the hall. "There's detergent and dryer sheets on the shelf there."

Tristan waved as he kept walking. Something white fell from the pile and fell to the ground. Maddox picked it up and noticed writing on a piece of motel paper. "Hey you dropped this."

Tristan finished turning on the washer and walked back to grab the paper. "The manager gave it to me. I forgot about it with everything that happened. It's a description of the people who were coming around looking for me." He trailed off as he studied the paper. "Shit, look at this." He handed the paper to Maddox. "That description match anyone you can think of?"

Maddox read the notes. The first two descriptions fit Billy and Brick perfectly. The third one was a man that had stayed in his car. "White man in his sixties, bald with a silver beard." He glanced at Tristan, "You don't think..."

Tristan shrugged. "It makes me wonder, that's for sure. I'd hope he wouldn't have been that stupid, but..." He smiled as he tapped the paper, "We can run that license plate and see what turns up. With luck, it'll be registered to the asshat."

Maddox was stunned. If the Chief of Police was behind the attempted murder of one of his cops, it was going to totally upend their department. But why would he want to get rid of Tristan?

"I think first thing tomorrow we have a thorough background check run on the Chief. Maybe something will pop and blow the case wide open. Cole can be discreet, right? I don't want to spook Bouchard anymore than we already have."

"Cole is insanely good at his job. No one will know he ran anything on the Chief."

"Guys, let's go. Movie time." Tallie yelled from the couch.

"Pushy little thing isn't she." Tristan smiled as he made his way to the living room.

Maddox turned off the kitchen light, then joined them on the couch. He glanced over and watched as Tallie and Tristan argued over what to watch. His heart constricted. This really was not going to be fun when they both left. His place was going to feel so empty when they were gone.

Maddox gasped awake and blinked rapidly, trying to figure out where he was. The living room was dark and Tristan was asleep with his head in Maddox's lap with a blanket pulled over him.

He picked up his phone to check the time. It was almost five a.m. Tallie must have tucked them in. Did he bother waking Tristan or just give him the last hour of sleep before their alarms went off?

After a few minutes of listening to Tristan's soft snoring, Maddox reached down and lightly brushed the hair back from the other man's forehead. He was embarrassed to notice his hand shaking. Why did such a simple act seem incredibly intimate?

He got a little more nerve and brushed the back of his hand down Tristan's cheek. He sighed and turned into his embrace. The movement was firm enough for Maddox to realize Tristan's head was directly over his rapidly growing erection. For a brief second, he considered brushing the other cheek to see if he could get his head moving back and forth, but decided that was just wrong, even if it was going to feel really good.

Tristan groaned in his sleep and nuzzled closer. Maddox gritted his teeth at the sexy sound.

He had to remind himself he was a gentleman, even if he didn't always act like it. He tucked his hands behind his head and laid still. It was going to be a painfully long forty-five minutes as he waited for Tristan to wake up.

Maddox's head snapped up when his phone finally went off. He needed Tristan as far away from his groin as possible or they were going to have a problem. He was going to need a seriously long, cold shower before work if he had any hope of getting through the day.

Tristan stretched as he woke slowly. "Morning."

Maddox mumbled morning back gruffly.

Tristan's eyes flew open as he looked up into Maddox's eyes, "Um... hi."

Maddox didn't move a muscle. "I guess we fell asleep during the movie and Tallie just left us like this."

"Okay, but how did I end up laying with my head snuggled up to your cock? I was on the other side of the couch."

"Subconscious wishful thinking?"

Tristan rolled his eyes and laughed, "Asshole."

"Hey, you are the one taking advantage of me here. I was asleep, and you cuddled up on me."

"Sorry if I offended your virtue." Tristan scowled as he sat up and moved so there was a cushion between them. "Didn't mean to make you uncomfortable."

"I was fine. You were the one that was stuck on a rock-hard pillow."

"Explains the dream at least." Tristan mumbled softly.

"Was it at least a nice-sized pillow?"

"Fuck if I know I was asleep, remember?"

"Plead the fifth, that's fine. I know you were cuddling up against me." Maddox knew he was playing with fire, but he couldn't resist. In fact, it was getting harder and harder to resist his new partner.

Tallie walked out of the bedroom with a mumbled morning as she went by them into the kitchen. "You really need a place with more than one bedroom and bathroom. Getting up before the sun is bullshit."

Tristan jumped to his feet and raced into the now empty bedroom.

Maddox stretched as he walked into the kitchen and turned on the coffeemaker. "This place has been the perfect size for me up to now. I'll make sure to get a bigger place next time I move."

Tallie handed him an empty mug. "What's with Tristan? He sure ran out of here fast."

Maddox glanced at the closed bedroom door. "I guess he couldn't handle being this close to my sexiness."

Tallie made a gagging sound as she grabbed the cereal out of the pantry. "You are so gross."

Maddox chuckled. It was too easy to make her blush.

"You guys are cute together. Think anything will happen between you?"

Maddox did not want to have this conversation with her or anyone. He didn't do relationships, especially not with someone he worked with. No matter how attracted he was to Tristan, he didn't think they could actually make anything happen. "We're partners, that's all. Besides, he's been a supe for like a week. He has a lot of his own shit to work out. I don't need that drama."

Tallie paused as she walked by him. "The gentleman doth protest too much."

Maddox's eyes widened. "How in the hell do you know Shakespeare?"

She rolled her eyes at him. "I'm homeless, not stupid. Stereotype much?"

As they finished eating, Tristan came out fully dressed. He brushed past Maddox on his way into the kitchen.

Maddox sighed. Why was everything so difficult between them? "I'll grab a quick shower, then we can get to the office."

He dug around his closet, then went and took the coldest shower he could muster.

The living room was quiet except for the sound of the t.v. Tristan and Tallie were watching. "All set. Let's get to the office and dig into these files."

It had taken everything he had the night before to not skip the movie and start reading right away. He wouldn't do that to Tallie though. As they left the condo, he prayed the clue to finding the kids were going to be in the human files and these families' nightmares would finally be over.

CHAPTER

Twenty~One

THE RIDE IN WAS SILENT. Tristan took the time to regroup and get back on track. The kids needed to be his only focus right now. His partner and his playboy ways weren't his concern. He nodded hellos to their team as he made his way through the pod until he stopped beside Cole's office.

"Morning."

Cole spun in his chair and smiled. "Hey, what's up?"

Tristan nodded to the chair opposite him. "Can I sit for a minute?"

"Sure, Reed is running a bit late today, so it's open." Cole cocked his head and studied Tristan. "You okay? You seem off."

"It's nothing." Tristan said as he sat down, "I need you to run a deep background check on someone for me."

Cole smirked. "A love interest of yours?"

"Not even close, my former Chief." Tristan huffed out a laugh and shook his head. "Do you guys really do that though? Look into your prospective partners like that?"

Cole shrugged. "In our line of work you can never be too careful."

Tristan nodded, "Yeah, I guess so."

"So," Cole cleared his throat and glanced around. "Why are we looking into him, and is this official or unofficial?"

"Would it change things depending on the answer?"

"Not really," Cole replied quickly. "If it's official though, we should let Vic know just to cover our asses."

"His name came up in regards to our two suspects, and a person matching his description was seen at my motel. So, yes, it's official." Tristan stood and moved to the door. "I'll let you know once he's given it the green light if you want."

"Sure, I'm going to start anyway though," Cole

said as he started typing on his computer. "If he's a suspect, we're all good."

Tristan nodded as he headed across the small space and into his own office.

Maddox was standing at the whiteboard where the timeline was drawn out, writing furiously. "I'm adding the dates and victim info to ours so we can see if anything stands out."

Tristan nodded and pulled his chair around to face the board. Once Maddox was done, he stepped back and stared at the board.

Maddox tapped his chin. "They alternate between human kid then paranormal kid, over and over."

Tristan nodded. "Each time the kids are the same age and sex, too. But no other similarities. Other than the two youngest being taken from bed; all the others were out doing normal activities." Tristan hesitated and then asked, "Do you think they're becoming more brazen by entering the homes or was there a specific reason they chose those?"

Maddox walked to the door and whistled. "Vic, come check this out."

Vic crossed the pod and stood next to the pair.

Maddox pointed toward the timeline. "We got the human files. Look how they lineup. They have to be connected." He glanced at Tristan and shrugged. "Hard to say on the two youngest, but given their ages, it might also be that there was never an opportunity to get them alone out in public."

"I don't recall seeing anything in the files on the kids connecting them other than the two who went to the same school. They didn't know each other and had no friends in common." Tristan grabbed the files and then pointed to the two kids he was referring to. "At their ages, they would have led completely separate lives."

Vic nodded and turned to face the two of them. "Care to tell me how you got these files when I've been stonewalled over and over?"

"I still have a few friends on the force. By the way, if word gets out about him helping us, he'll be screwed. I know we don't take on humans, but if that changes..." Tristan trailed off with a shrug.

Maddox nodded in agreement. "He'd make a good agent."

Vic smiled. "I'll keep that in mind. Cole mentioned he was looking into the chief. what's that about?"

"The two assailants' only connection is that he was their arresting officer on multiple occasions. And the motel manager provided a description of the two of them and a third man who sat in his car. It could be him." Tristan handed the slip of paper to Vic and waited.

"It's vague, but it might be enough to use. Have you run the plate of the car yet?"

Tristan shook his head, "No, that's on the list to do, though. When we met with him yesterday, he didn't give anything away, but my gut is telling me he's hiding something. Plus, he's personally handling my case and won't give me any details. It's off, and not standard protocol."

"Well, you guys better figure out something soon. If the pattern holds true, you only have a couple of days until the next human kid is taken." All three men turned to find Kiely leaning against the doorjamb.

They turned back to the wall.

Maddox shook his head. "Five days between the first and second set, eight days between the next two, nine days between the last two sets. So we can assume the next set will be ten days later, which will be the 17th and 18th. That gives us four days to figure something out."

Kiely walked forward and held her hand out. "Give me the plate you want run and I'll work the background check with Cole while you guys finish reading the human's files. This way you don't lose time on either case."

Tristan handed her the paper with the details. "You're a lifesaver."

She winked as she backed out of the office.

Maddox paced in front of the wall. "What about getting the families together? Maybe putting them all together like that and talking will jog something loose and we can find a connection that alone they wouldn't have thought of. But hearing someone else mention it might trigger an ah-ha moment."

They turned and looked at Vic for permission. He pursed his lips as he thought about it. "I have no doubt our families will come. Not sure if the human ones will but since I couldn't even get the files from TPD, I don't see them helping us with this anyway. We can give it a shot."

"If I was in their shoes and somebody offered me even the slightest hope, I'd jump at it," Tristan replied as he pulled out his phone and started texting. "But I think I can get Jaylen to help with that. It might be good to have it come from a human police officer."

Maddox blew out a breath, "There's not much chance he won't get burned for this. It will get out and he will lose his job over it. Make sure he's aware of the consequences."

"He's free and going to call me in a minute. From what I know of him, which isn't much I'll admit, he'll do anything to help with the kids."

Tristan's phone rang, and he held up a finger as he answered. "Hey Jaylen, thanks for calling so quickly. I've got you on speaker with Maddox and ASAC Judge."

"Oh, okay, yeah, sure, no problem."

"We've been looking at the files you gave us and we noticed something pretty significant. There is no doubt the two cases are connected in a big way. We just can't figure out why yet."

"Really, wow." Jaylen paused for a moment. "I'm glad to hear that the files are helping, but if you've got your boss on the line, I know there's more than what you're telling me."

Vic smiled, "You're right, I know what we're going to ask of you is going to put your career with the TPD on the line. We'll understand if you can't help."

"Just tell me. If I can help find the kids, I'm all in. They are more important. It's why I joined the force in the first place after all. To make a difference and to help those who need it."

"We want to get the parents of the missing human kids to meet with the paranormal parents here. Our thought is to get them talking and see if anything comes up that might help." Tristan explained.

"You want me to approach them then?" Jaylen questioned, "It makes sense, of course I'll do it. Tell me when and where to have them meet and I'll do my best."

"Thanks man, I'll text you the information."

Maddox blew out a breath after they hung up. "That kid has balls, I'll give him that. Not sure I'd risk so much when I was a rookie. We gotta do right by him if something bad happens."

Vic nodded. "We will. Even if it's not with us, we'll make sure he has somewhere to go. Now, you guys finish going through those files. Get as much detail as you can while I clear the big conference room for this evening."

Maddox plopped down in his chair and grabbed half the file folders. "Let's dig in."

The alarm on Tristan's phone startled them both from their scrutiny of the files. "I've got to go meet

Dr. Obinski. It shouldn't take long. I'll text you when I'm done and see what the plan is from there."

Maddox waved without looking up from the file in front of him. "Sounds good. I'll keep plugging away while you're gone."

Tristan made the short drive to the hospital and Dr. Obinski's office. The receptionist greeted him and told him to have a seat. He looked around the tastefully decorated waiting room as he waited. Within a few minutes, a nurse called his name and ushered him into one of the exam rooms.

"The doctor will be with you shortly." She said as she closed the door on her way out.

Tristan frowned as he glanced around the room. He'd never been to an appointment where they didn't do some routine checks, like weight, blood pressure, and things like that. Did paranormals do things differently, he wondered?

He'd just peeked out the small window when the sound of the door behind him had him whirling around in surprise. "That was quick."

Dr. Obinski smiled. "I'm not really seeing patients today, so I was ready when they told me you'd arrived. How are you feeling?"

Tristan shrugged, "Pretty damn good, actually.

Still adjusting to having wings and shit, but health wise, I feel fine."

"Yeah, I can only imagine how different that must be for you. Have you noticed anything unusual? Appetite changed or sleep patterns?"

"Other than alcohol not working anymore?" Tristan grinned. "I jumped right back into work on a big case, so I haven't really had the time to sit down and think about that kind of stuff. Should I be worried?"

Dr. Obinski quickly shook his head. "Not at all. Those were just routine questions so I can get an idea of how you're adjusting, nothing more. You'll find that you might have a higher metabolism now and will require more calories to help fuel your abilities, but it's normal for us."

Tristan's phone buzzed in his pocket repeatedly. "Sorry doc, let me check why my phone is blowing up."

He unlocked the phone to find several messages from Maddox.

911... check your phone

I'm at the hospital

Open your phone

We need to talk to the doc.

I'm in the waiting room now.

Come get me!

Tristan snorted. "Apparently, my partner is in the waiting room and is desperate to talk to us. Do you have time for me to bring him back?"

Dr. Obinski looked surprised. "Um sure, we can bring him back." He walked to the door and opened it. "Sandy, can you get the man in the waiting room and bring him to my office? We'll be right there."

He turned back to Tristan. "Follow me. Let's see what the big emergency is."

Dr. Obinski pointed to one of the chairs in front of a large wooden desk and then sat behind it.

A few seconds later, Maddox rushed in with a file in his hand. "I'm sorry to interrupt your appointment, but we got some info that I think Dr. Obinski can help with, so I wanted to catch you while you guys were together."

"Help with what?" Tristan asked in confusion. "I've been over those files with a fine- tooth comb. What the hell did I miss?"

"Nothing. This isn't about the kids. This is from the background that came back on the Chief," Maddox said as he pulled a piece of paper out of the folder he carried and placed it on the desk. "Doc, can you explain what this is? I've never heard of it and when I did a search on Google, it was a bit too technical for me to understand."

"Maddox?" Tristan growled in frustration. "What is this about?"

"Your old Chief has a niece who is dying of some weird disease and I was hoping your doctor could help explain things."

"And this is 911? Why does that matter to what's going on?"

"Like I said, I did a bit of searching and what little I could understand had my gut screaming to pay attention. This disease only affects humans, but all paranormals have it if I'm reading it right."

Dr. Obinski nodded his head. "Yes, that's correct. It's an extremely rare disease. Only one in one hundred thousand people are affected by it. Debilitas Noctis or Weakness of the Night is ultimately a death sentence for all who have it."

Tristan glanced at Maddox. "Weird, I've never heard of it either. How do humans get the disease?"

"We don't know why some humans get sick and others don't. The most they know about it is it's a latent paranormal gene and when the realms collided, the blast of radiation malformed that gene.

What they can't figure out is why even all these years later babies are still being born with the malformation, some to families that didn't have it to begin with. There is no rhyme or reason as to which ones have the bad gene and which ones don't."

"So that's why they started doing genetic testing on all human babies at birth?"

"Precisely." Dr. Obinski nodded as he skimmed over the sheet in his hands. "This poor child doesn't have long left. Once the disease has manifested, death comes swiftly."

"If this is such a horrific death, why don't more people know about it?" Maddox asked.

"The ratio of those affected is so small that people tend to not pay attention until it affects them or a loved one. There are only a handful of research studies even being done in regards to this disease. Currently, in Florida, there are just over twenty-two million people living here. Of those, only about two thousand have the abnormal gene."

Tristan gaped in shock, "That's crazy, so these people are just left to die?"

"Without funding, I'm afraid scientists can't do much."

"When you say paranormal gene, does that mean that those people could become paranormal under the right circumstances like Tristan did?" Maddox questioned.

Dr. Obinski shrugged. "Honestly, we really don't know. Like I said before, there are only a handful of cases of this happening. Humans are so afraid of more of them being turned that they do everything in their power to keep our kinds separated. They gained power after the fusion because they outnumbered and outgunned us. If we start changing humans to paranormals, there would be all-out war."

Tristan frowned. "I get that, but I'm still confused about what all this has to do with the Chief and my case?"

Maddox leaned forward excitedly. "Don't you see, they don't know why you changed. And his niece is dying from a paranormal gene. What if he thinks you are the key to curing her?"

"That's fucking insane, but I can see that. When people are desperate, they do weird shit." Tristan agreed.

"Dr. Obinski, I have a question for you about me before you go." Tristan turned his attention back to the doc. "I transformed because I have a latent paranormal gene, you said. But we were talking the other day and realized something that didn't make sense to us."

"I'll try to answer if I can."

"If all babies, human and paranormal, are genetically tested at birth, wouldn't it be known that I had this latent gene?"

"Yes," Dr. Obinski agreed, "That's the thing. All humans have it, it's not something that's advertised, but every single person has it. It's the same gene that when it's broken or malformed causes Weakness of the Night."

Maddox frowned. "So are you saying that because every human has this latent gene, they could potentially be changed like Tristan was?"

"We don't know exactly what caused his transformation. It's not like we can test humans to see what makes them change obviously. So we can only hypothesize on how it all works." Dr. Obinski stood up. "I hope you guys don't mind, but I need to get back to the hospital. If you have any more questions, feel free to give me a call. I'll give you my personal cell number."

Tristan smiled as he stood up and offered his hand, "Thanks Doc, and if you're open to new patients, maybe I'll transfer into your care."

"I do, and I'd be happy to have you. Good luck with your case."

Tristan and Maddox thanked him and headed outside, both lost in their thoughts of all the information they'd just been given.

"Is everything lined up for meeting the families?" Tristan asked as they got to their vehicles.

"Yeah, they should be arriving soon."

"Can we have a drink when we get home tonight, even if Tallie is there? Cause I think we're going to need it after this."

"Tallie will probably offer to play bartender. Drinks are good with me and don't think I didn't notice you called it home. Maybe I do need to start looking for a bigger place like Tallie suggested." Maddox winked at Tristan.

"Slip of the tongue, you know what I meant."

"You are welcome to slip your tongue any time you want."

"I don't even know how to respond to that."

"First a tongue slip and now tongue tied. I see a theme with you."

Tristan frowned as he climbed into his truck. He couldn't keep up with Maddox and his mood swings. Hot then cold, back and forth until Tristan was going insane trying to figure shit out. It was exhausting and frustrating.

CHAPTER
Twenty~Two

MADDOX STOOD at the door to the conference room and shook hands with each family as they walked in. Jaylen had come and was helping convince the humans to go inside. It was probably the first time in their lives to enter a paranormal building.

Tristan walked up with Vic and stared around the full room. "Wow, rookie actually got them all to come."

Vic walked to the podium. Tristan, Maddox, and Jaylen lined up behind him. "Thank you all for coming. I know this is highly unusual. Since March 12th eight children have gone missing, four human, and four paranormal. We've just become aware of this detail and it gives us new hope of finding out where your children are."

A human man in the back stood up. "Where are all the human cops? Why aren't they leading this?"

Vic sighed. "Cooperation between the agencies isn't optimal. We are sharing our information with them and have offered to coordinate a joint task force with them. Thanks to Officer Rose," He waved toward Jaylen, "He was the key to helping us figure out the two cases were connected.

Maddox leaned toward Tristan and whispered. "There's no way the kid is going to get out of this scot free."

Tristan nodded.

Vic continued, "This is going to sound highly unusual, and it is, but our situation dictates it." He clicked a button and a large screen lit up on the wall next to them. "This is a timeline showing when and where each of your children was taken. We want to have an open dialogue with all of you in the hopes that with this new information, we see something that may have been missed before."

Everyone stood and rushed closer to the screen. They all talked at once. Some cried as they saw their child's information.

Each tear was a gut punch to Maddox. It was his

failure to solve the case that had so many of them here grieving.

Maddox walked among the families, listening as they shared stories of their children. It gave him hope that maybe someday the two sides could learn to live in harmony. Mothers were hugging mothers. Fathers cried as they showed off pictures of their kids. Human or paranormal didn't matter right now. The only thing that did was their missing kids.

An hour later, as Maddox was reaching his limit of emotional turmoil for the evening, the families started filing out.

Vic walked up and clapped him on the back. "That was great. I don't think we got anything valuable out of it, but I saw humans and paranormals exchanging phone numbers and emails. Maybe there's hope for us yet."

He turned to Jaylen and held out a hand. "You did good, kid. I've already promised the guys we'd look out for you. If you get any blowback, let us know."

Jaylen smiled shyly as he turned and left.

Maddox laid a hand on Tristan's shoulder. "Ready to get home, honey?"

Vic quirked an eyebrow at them. "Care to fill me in?"

Tristan elbowed Maddox's rock hard stomach and flinched. "He's being an ass. I'm staying at his place for a few days while he has a houseguest."

"Don't make it sound so innocent. We are sharing a bed, after all."

"What is wrong with you?" Tristan whispered angrily. "Sir, it's not what he's making it sound like. I swear."

Vic shook his head as he laughed loudly. "Maddox and I have known each other for a very long time. I know exactly what it sounds like and what it is. Don't worry, your secret is safe with me."

Tristan groaned as he threw his head back, "Fuck my life. He's got everyone buying his bullshit." Tristan glared at Maddox, "I thought the bathroom or bars were your thing. You take a lot of guys home, that this is a normal thing for you?"

Maddox slid his arm around Tristan's shoulders and pulled him close. "Baby, I don't care where I am. If there's a nice piece of ass and I'm interested, you know I'm going for it." He reached back and slapped Tristan's ass. "And your ass is mighty fine."

Tristan's jaw fell open.

Maddox shoved him away playfully. "God, you are too easy to tease. Relax man, your virtue is safe with me."

Tristan rolled his eyes as he pushed his way past. "Fucking asshole, teases until I say something and then it's time to run for the hills like a virgin on their wedding night."

"Come on honey, Tallie's waiting for us."

Maddox played it off like he had been kidding, but really, he hadn't. At some point, he'd softened enough toward Tristan to realize what an amazing man he was. And his ass really was fine. It could just be that he hadn't gotten laid since Tristan came into his life, or maybe he really was starting to fall for him.

Vic held the door open for them. "I don't care what goes on in the privacy of your home. Just make sure you guys are on time for work. Kinky sex is not a valid excuse for missing a shift."

Maddox threw back his head and laughed at the look of horror on Tristan's face. Humans really were prudes. Guess they don't tease each other as openly as paranormals did.

Maddox tapped on the steering wheel, waiting for the light to turn red. "Shit, food." He grabbed his phone and called Tallie.

"Hello?"

"Hey, Tristan and I are on our way. What do you want us to pick up for dinner?"

"Actually, it's all taken care of. It's ready when you get here."

He wasn't sure if he should be impressed or scared. *"We're only five minutes away, so see you in a few."*

He hung up and switched to a text to Tristan.

> Maddox: Tallie says she has dinner ready. Don't worry, there's an ER only ten minutes away.

> Tristan: Something tells me we are in good hands tonight. No worries.

"At least someone is confident," Maddox grumbled as he gunned the engine as the light turned green.

A few minutes later, they pulled into their usual parking spots. Maddox waited for Tristan to catch up before going inside. "I don't know about you, but today has been a serious mind melt. I really hope Tallie doesn't want to watch another movie. I am ready for bed as soon as dinner's done." It might also be that he normally spent sixteen hours of his day alone and in the last four days, he hadn't had a moment to himself.

"She's been home alone all day. What are the chances she won't want company, old man?"

"Old man, pfft, I'm only two years your senior."

They took the elevator up to his condo. "Tallie, we're home," he called out as they entered. Two heads popped out from the kitchen. "Mom, what are you doing here?"

Marta held her arms out and gave him a hug. "Well, Tristan reached out to me about Tallie. He thought it would be nice for me to come meet her."

Maddox glanced at Tristan. He wasn't sure if he should be pissed at the other man for meddling. He'd helped a lot of people over the years without getting his mother involved. Not that he was trying to protect her. He didn't know why he kept this part of himself a secret.

She grabbed his chin and made him look at her. "You're a good boy with a big heart. Tallie's told me all about what you've done for her."

Tallie bounced up and down behind them. "Your mom told me all about your house and said if I wanted, I could come stay with her for a while. She'd even help me get enrolled in school over there."

Maddox's jaw dropped. "You know she lives among ogres, right? Have you ever met one?"

They all gave each other confused glances. "You are an ogre, are you not?" Marta asked sternly.

Maddox rolled his eyes. "That's not what I meant. You know the purebreds are a lot more aggressive than I am. Are you sure she'll be okay there? And why do you want a kid hanging around?" He glanced at Tallie. "No offense. She's just been on her own for the last sixteen years."

"Maybe that's why she wants her around. Ever think she could be lonely? Not everyone wants to be isolated." Tristan said as he leaned against the wall with his arms crossed and gave Maddox a pointed look.

Maddox glared at Tristan. "If she were lonely, she would have told me." He tried to sound certain, but he heard the question in his tone.

Marta grabbed his hand and pulled him toward the kitchen table. "I've been very happy, but I also think it would be nice to have someone to take care of again. Lord knows I thought I'd have grand babies by now and since that doesn't look to be happening in the next few months..." she trailed off as she pushed him into the chair and went back to the kitchen.

"Does it make anyone want to laugh at the thought of Maddox sharing his space with a baby? I mean, he's the biggest playboy I've ever met, and he doesn't share his toys with anyone."

"Playboy?" Marta gasped at the same time Tallie giggled. "He's never brought anyone home before and never talks about anyone, so I just assumed he was keeping to himself. Maybe you're more like your dad than you think?"

Maddox's head snapped around. "What does that mean? Did he take advantage of you, then take off?"

Marta tsked. "He never gave me anything I didn't want."

Tristan snickered as Maddox choked on his own saliva. "Jesus mom."

She shrugged. "He comes around every once in a while. We have a good time, then he goes back to his realm. It's never bothered me one bit."

Maddox dropped his head into his hands. "Oh my god. I'm going to have nightmares for a month now."

Tallie patted him on the back. "Poor baby, just found out his mom has sex."

"Guess that apple didn't fall far from that tree at all." Tristan grinned at Tallie.

"I guess you have no issue imagining your parents doing it?" He hoped that disturbed Tristan. He didn't want to be the only one nauseated right now.

Tristan shrugged, "My father died a long time ago, but no, the thought doesn't gross me out. They were in love and wanted to express that physically."

"Gag me with a spoon," Maddox mumbled as Marta set a large roasted chicken down in the center of the table.

"It's the love part that freaked you out, isn't it?" Tristan grinned as he took a seat at the table across from Maddox. "It's a scary concept to care for someone and not just physical gratification.

"Believe it or not, I do want to settle down and have a family..." He froze, realizing what he'd said. He'd never admitted that out loud before and now he declared it in front of his new partner, his mother, and a teen prostitute. He snorted, thinking that sounded like the start of a bad joke. "I just mean, love is great if you can find it."

He dug into the bowl of mashed potatoes, praying they would drop the subject and move on. He blew out a breath when it seemed Tristan took the hint.

"So, is it a go? Are you two going to be roommates?"

Tallie glanced at Marta, waiting. Marta reached out and grabbed her hand. "You are welcome when you're ready. Heck, you can come home with me tonight if you want?"

Tallie glanced at Maddox, a question on her face.

He nodded. "I'll go along with whatever you decide. If you want to go tonight, I won't be upset."

She turned back to Marta. "I would love to go with you tonight. Not that living with these two isn't a dream, but I'm all for not having to get up at sunrise so they can get to the shower before work."

Marta clapped her hands. "It's settled then. After dinner, we'll clean up and get out of your hair."

Maddox smiled, but inside he was a little sad. The small world he'd had thrust on him over the last week was shrinking again, and he didn't know if he was ready for it. He knew it was stupid to be upset. She wouldn't be that far away. He could visit anytime. He had to. He had to make sure the ogres didn't take advantage of the tiny sprite. Hell, if they could ever solve the case, he'd take a week off and go stay with them. He couldn't remember the last time he'd had a vacation. This was honestly the first time he could remember wanting one.

CHAPTER
Twenty-Three

TRISTAN WIPED his hands on the dishrag as he listened to the now silent apartment. He'd offered to do the dishes while the other three helped Tallie get her things, then they all said goodbye.

"They're gone." Maddox sighed as he walked into the kitchen and grabbed a beer out of the fridge.

"I think I'm going to be heading out too, then." Tristan tossed the towel onto the counter and turned to face Maddox. "You were wanting an early night, too."

Maddox leaned against the counter and picked at the label of his beer bottle. "I mean, after that insane dinner conversation, I'm pretty awake. If you want to hang for a bit, that's cool with me."

Tristan bit his lip and glanced around as he

thought about what to do. He loved being around his partner, but it was like slow torture at the same time. He took one look at the naked longing in Maddox's eyes and nodded, "Yeah man. Let's see if there is anything good on tv. Oh, and thanks for offering me a beer."

Maddox grabbed a beer, then made his way to the couch. "You were technically in the kitchen first. You could have gotten one for both of us."

"It's your house. You should be waiting on me hand and foot." Tristan smirked as he sat on the couch and kicked his feet up on the coffee table.

"You've used my shower and slept on top of me. I think we're long past guest status, don't you?"

"Well, when you put it that way." Tristan laughed, "And the sleeping on you thing, I already explained. You make everything sound so tawdry." He grabbed the remote and flipped through the channels. "So... about what you said earlier at dinner."

Maddox groaned and laid his head back against the couch, staring up at the ceiling.

"Did you mean it? Do you really want that? A family and to settle down with someone?" Tristan took a sip of his beer as he studied Maddox out of the corner of his eye. "Or was it just a line for your mom?"

"Up until I said it, I would have said it was a line, but as the words came out, I realized they were true. It's not that I never thought about having a family, but the longer I've been alone, the less I've thought about it." He blew out a breath and rolled his head toward Tristan. "Having you guys in my place was a wake-up call. I guess that I'm not getting any younger and I actually enjoyed having you guys around."

Tristan nodded. "I get that. My mom is all I have left and even she is gone most days. When I visit her, she rarely remembers me. It's hard to be alone, day in and day out. You watch people meet and fall in love, start their families and you wonder what's so wrong with you that you can't find that for yourself. I had a great job, had what I thought were great friends and now I'm in a rent by the hour motel."

"That's just it right, it's not you. I believe in fate, which means fate hasn't shown me my other half yet. I know it will happen one day. I'm a good person. The fates wouldn't let me die alone."

Tristan smirked, "No offense, but something tells me you won't find them in the bathrooms." He paused and then let out a sigh. "I'm sorry. I was going for a joke and that was wrong. I'm just a bit out of sorts and I took it out on you.... Even if you did only pick up men that way."

"I get it. You aren't pointing out anything that isn't true." He blew out a breath and stared back up at the ceiling. "What about you? Do you believe in fate and having another half out there somewhere?"

"After seeing the love that my parents shared every day they were together, yes, wholeheartedly. There is no way they weren't made for each other. Even when they bickered and fought, you could feel the love and affection they had for one another." He took another sip of his rapidly warming bottle and then set it down on the table. "Fate though, I'm not sure. Why would they let two people so perfect together get separated so quickly? She's had to live without him and now all she has is her memories. That seems cruel to me, you know."

"I see your point, but maybe you should look at it like they were special. They actually found their other half and, however brief a time it was, was still amazing and magical. It's not fair. It was such a short time, but they experienced what many people don't and that is worth something, I think."

"I guess I never really thought of it that way." Tristan smiled, "So, you believe in fate and that your other half is out there. But how do you know when you've found them? What if you did and you let them go?"

"You know you've found them when the idea of them leaving you or dying takes the breath from your lungs and the color from your world. When you know you don't want to live without that person, you know they are your person." He shrugged. "If you are crazy enough to let them go, it's never too late to make things right and get them back. If it's real, you'll find a way to be together again."

"So your plan is to put your potential mate in a life-threatening position to see how you react." Tristan winked as he stood up and headed to the kitchen. "Harsh, man. That's really harsh."

"Honestly, just thinking about something bad happening should be enough to scare the shit out of you and make you realize you don't want to be without them." He let out a loud growl. "Jesus, what is wrong with me? I'm waxing on poetically and really I'm just a meathead who likes quickies in a bar. Ignore everything I just said. I told you I'm mentally done for the night and now you see it's true."

Tristan glanced over his shoulder and shook his

head. "Nope, just getting hotter and hotter." He mumbled to himself as he entered the kitchen.

Tristan groaned as he stretched and hit a warm body. His eyes jerked open as he took in the unfamiliar ceiling. Logically he knew it had to be Maddox beside him, and he had been sharing the couch bed with him, but that didn't account for where he was now.

"How did I get into your bed?" Tristan asked with a yawn.

Maddox ran his hands down his face as he yawned. "We were pretty buzzed last night, so we agreed you would crash here. We had fallen asleep on the couch and I woke up at three a.m. with a neck cramp, so I woke you up and we came in here. I figured no reason for us to be sore from sleeping weird."

"The last thing I need is for Vic to question why I'm walking funny after yesterday." Tristan laughed as he rolled his head to the side to look into Maddox's eyes. "Morning, by the way."

"Morning. I know I give you a lot of shit in front of Vic but trust me, he is one of my closest friends and he knows I'm just fucking around with you." He chewed his lip for a minute as he stared up at the ceiling. "Any chance you were so buzzed last night that you don't remember my drunken ramblings?"

"That's the problem, you fucking around with me." Tristan joked as he grabbed his phone to check the time. "And I don't think you were rambling at all. It ... You...." Tristan blew out a breath and tried again, "It showed me a different side of you. Not just the playboy persona, but the man beneath. I liked it."

Maddox grabbed his pillow from behind his head and smashed it against his face. "Can we just pretend you didn't see that side? That part of me is weak and I don't like it." He mumbled.

Tristan pulled at the pillow unsuccessfully. "Stop being an idiot. It's hot to see a strong man be vulnerable and in touch with his softer side. You are one kick-ass, scary mother fucker when you want to be. But that's not all you are. If you let people see that side of you more often, those quickies might turn into actual dates. You just have to take those damn walls down a bit."

"Thanks for the life advice, Dr. Phil." He tossed the pillow aside and sat up on the side of the bed. His back to Tristan.

"At the risk of ruining this moment, I'm going to take a shower. And no, that is not an invitation for you to join me."

"Spoilsport." Maddox mumbled. "I'll get coffee going while you're in there."

Tristan smirked as he grabbed some clean clothes and headed into the bathroom. As soon as the door was shut and he could relax his tense shoulders, he cringed at the sentimental shit that he'd spewed. Not that he hadn't meant every word, but Maddox wasn't the type to appreciate that kind of stuff. He was locked in his imaginary box of having to be a man's man and not letting any perceived weakness see the light of day.

He dropped his clothes on the counter and turned on the water to a lukewarm temperature. Waking up next to the sexy ass bastard had left him hard and wanting. But that didn't mean he was willing to take a cold shower. Life was too short for that crap.

"Hurry up, I need one too."

Tristan grinned at his words and what a different meaning they had after what he'd just been thinking. "Yeah, yeah." He called out as he climbed in to take the quickest shower he could.

Ten minutes later he walked out of the bathroom

with a towel wrapped around his hips as water dripped down his chest. "I'll get dressed out here so you can get in the shower."

Tristan frowned as he watched Maddox move past him without making eye contact. He turned so he could see the other man as he shut the bathroom door. "What the fuck?" He whispered into the empty room.

As he got dressed, he absently went over what all had happened that morning trying to justify his partner's weird behavior. He made his way to the kitchen and grabbed two mugs out of the cabinet. He filled the cups and added sugar to his and left Maddox's black. As the other man came around the corner, he held up the steaming nectar of the gods. "Black, right?"

"Thanks. I might need three more just to shake off last night. Why I thought it was okay to drink that much on a work night is beyond me. I've never gone to work hungover." He grabbed the cup from Tristan. "I'll make sure Vic knows you are the bad influence."

"You're a bastard." Tristan chuckled as he grabbed his keys and wallet. "Maybe I'll spread a rumor that you're not the god in bed you think you are. Might as well have fun with this if you're going to keep implying we're sleeping together anyway."

"So you think I haven't slept with half the office already... interesting." He shrugged as he brushed past Tristan.

Tristan frowned as he moved to the door. He hoped that was another one of his jokes, but with what he knew of Maddox's playboy behavior, he couldn't be sure. And it would explain why Vic didn't bat an eye at his antics. If he'd already proved he could keep things separate and not let it interfere with work.

"Since all your stuff is still here, do you just want to ride together to save on gas?" Maddox asked as he paused next to the driver's side door of Scarlet.

Tristan hesitated before finally nodding and pocketing his keys. If nothing else, it would give him a chance to think and not have to pay attention to the road. He pulled open the passenger door and climbed in, careful not to leave a scuff on the beautiful car's interior.

Once they were both in with their seatbelts fastened, Maddox started the car. "Do you want to grab something to eat on the way in? We can go through a fast-food joint or grab something at a bakery if you want?"

"Sure, let's get something close to the office, though. I don't want any crumbs or shit to get in Scarlet's interior."

"I know just the place," Maddox assured him as he pulled out into traffic.

Tristan stared out his side window as he tried to piece together the puzzle that was Maddox. Every time he thought he'd had him figured out, a new facet would come to the surface and change his whole perspective. Maddox the playboy, Maddox the agent, Maddox the knight in shining armor, Maddox the family guy. What other side would emerge next?

They drove through Ybor and stopped at a food truck. Maddox grabbed his wallet and handed him a $20. "Mrs. Diaz never lets me pay. If you order on your own and pay, maybe she'll take your money."

Tristan scrunched his eyebrows at him in a what the hell look before he took the money and put it in his pocket.

He followed Maddox across the parking lot and got in line.

"Hola Maddox, it's been a few days. I was starting to think you found somewhere new to eat." A tiny Hispanic woman yelled over the heads of everyone in front of them.

Maddox waved her off. "Just busy with a case. I would never cheat on you."

When it was their turn, the woman leaned on the counter and gave them a big smile. "Those boys who keep giving me trouble came by the other day and I mentioned that I had called you and they took off." She cackled. "And who is this handsome man you've brought with you?"

"This is my new partner, Tristan."

She leaned on her toes and looked him up and down. "Haven't seen you around before. Did you just move here?"

Maddox leaned close. "He was human two weeks ago."

She gasped and studied Tristan again. "Well, then that means you haven't had the best Cuban food in the state. I'll make a bag of all of Maddox's favorite things for you to try." She turned away and then turned back. "And don't even think about paying. If you're with Maddox, your money's no good here."

Maddox let out a sigh. "Give me back the twenty."

Tristan laughed and handed it over. "Later, you gonna tell me what you did to earn that level of devotion from her?"

Maddox feigned shock. "I didn't do anything. Maybe I'm just an amazing person and she recognizes that." He scanned the line then went back to an older woman three back. They exchanged words for a minute, then he came back.

"The only way I get money to her is by having people buy extra stuff with my money, then they give it to the homeless group around the corner and, in return, they keep an eye on her for me."

Tristan gaped, "Maddox the philanthropist," He mumbled as he studied the people around them. "I can't figure you out man, and it's driving me fucking nuts."

Maddox shrugged. "I've been in their shoes. I've felt alone, scared, and hopeless. Besides, I have a lot of free time. I've spent a lot of time just walking the city and I met a lot of good people down on their luck. I'm just trying to make all our lives a little better."

"You know, if you'd let people see this side of you, they'd be in love with you in no time. You could have that family you want and not be so alone. You're like a male version of Mother Teresa, but way sexier." Tristan smiled at Mrs. Diaz as she leaned over the counter and handed him the bag. "Enjoy and don't be a stranger." She glanced at Maddox and waggled her finger at him. "He's nice, keep him, mijo."

Tristan bit his lip to keep from laughing as he turned and winked at Maddox. "Yeah, get your head out of your ass and keep me."

Maddox's mouth opened and closed several times. He turned on his heel and walked to the car without a word.

Tristan threw his head back and let out a loud belly laugh as he followed behind his partner. It was rare he was able to get one over on Maddox, so when he did, it made him feel like he'd won the lottery. He climbed into Scarlet and set the bag on the floor at his feet. "Looks like we've got enough food for the whole pod."

The ride to the office was quiet. They pulled into their parking spot and climbed out of the car, still not speaking. Tristan glanced at Maddox and debated if he'd said something wrong or if the other man was just lost in his head.

"That smells so good," Shepherd called out as they entered the pod.

"Good thing we brought enough for everyone," Tristan replied loud enough for everyone to hear. "Who wants breakfast on Maddox?"

"Can I have mine on a plate? No offense Maddox, but you're not my type." Ensley winked at him.

Tristan felt his cheeks heat up as he realized what he'd said and how it'd been taken. Thankfully, Kiely interrupted before he had to say anything.

"Hey, I got the results of the plate I ran for you guys." She said as she started shuffling the papers she was carrying and then began pulling things out of her pockets. With a laugh of triumph, she held up a small sticky note. "It belongs to a James Bouchard, white male, sixty-two lives in Carrollwood."

Tristan's jaw dropped as his head whipped around to face Maddox in shocked astonishment. "It really was him."

He'd kind of known it was, but to have that proof shocked the hell out of him.

Maddox shook his head. "I can't believe it actually is. It made sense, but it seemed like such a conspiracy theory. I guess I thought it wouldn't be."

Cole shrugged. "I'm just surprised he was stupid enough to use his own damn vehicle." He pulled the items out of the bag and set them on the table. "Thanks for the food, by the way."

Vic walked out of his office and grabbed a pastelitos and bit into it. "People in power tend to feel invincible." He said while his mouth was still full.

"Since we're all here, guess we should fill you all in on what happened and pick your brains a bit." Tristan sat down in a chair and pulled a pastry closer to him. "The ride here smelling all of this was torture."

"That's a Cangrejos," Maddox supplied with a smile as he sat down a few seats away and surveyed what items were left.

"Can you talk and eat or what?" Vic questioned as he took a bite of his breakfast and moaned at the delicious taste. "And feel free to bring this every day."

Tristan laughed. "We're working three cases. Two of them we've discovered are linked. The human and paranormal kids are connected, we just haven't figured out for sure how exactly. What we do know is that a human child gets abducted and the next day a paranormal kid of the same age and gender does as well. If the pattern holds true, we have three days until the next one is taken."

Maddox nodded. "We don't know why they're being taken, and none of the kids seem to have anything in common that we can find."

"But we also haven't had a chance to compare the

human kids with paranormal ones extensively." Tristan agreed, "I only had what I remembered from before my attack. Now that we have the files, we can do a more extensive comparison."

He waited for everyone to nod their under-standing before moving on. "The third case is the two guys we brought in for attacking me at the motel. Turns out they were hired by the Chief of TPD and my old boss. Yesterday, we met with Dr. Obinski. He's the doctor that treated me after I .... Shit, what's the right word?" He looked around help-lessly with a shrug.

"Joined the dark side?" Jasmina called out with a laugh.

Tristan laughed, "Sure, that works. Anyway, Cole found out that the Chief has a niece with an abnormal paranormal gene that is killing her. Dr. Obinski explained a bit more and the only thing we can figure out is that he was trying to capture me because of my transformation to the dark side. We think he's hoping to use me to save her somehow."

"A human with a paranormal gene?" Raelle frowned thoughtfully. "I've never heard of anything like that."

"It's called Debilitas Noctis, or Weakness of the Night. It's a latent gene that all humans have, only a handful have the abnormal variant, it kills 100% of those that have it though."

Vic leaned forward. "Wait, I overheard two of the human families talking about it the other night. I didn't pay attention to what they were saying. I just remember hearing that name and thinking it sounded kinda cool. I had no idea it had anything to do with our kind."

Maddox and Tristan exchanged glances.

"That seems awfully coincidental." Tristan frowned. "Yesterday, Dr. Obinski explained that there are only about two thousand cases in all of Florida."

Vic turned to Cross. "Can you and Raelle go through the kids' cases and compare them for anything connecting them?"

The two agents nodded and stood up to leave. "Yeah, just get us the files while we clear off some things from our desks." Raelle called.

"Ensley, Shephard, can you two look into this 'Weakness of the Night' and see what you can find out? One of the human families has a connection in some way to it."

They nodded and left the conference table with their pastries in hand.

"That leaves the two of you to deal with your old

Chief," Vic said as he turned to face Maddox and Tristan.

"Do we have enough evidence to arrest him, or at least bring him in for questioning?" Maddox asked as he leaned forward with his elbows resting on the table.

"You can't seriously think we can just waltz in and arrest him, do you?" Tristan gaped in shock. "Isn't there like some channels we have to go through, or hoops we have to jump through to get permission? The humans will freak out on us."

"Fuck that. He orchestrated an attack on a paranormal. That doesn't make him anything special, just another scumbag. Why should he be treated any differently?" Maddox crossed his arms angrily.

Vic laughed, "Tristan, stop thinking like a human cop. We don't answer to them. We have our own system and we hold people accountable, no matter their position. Cole, can you hack Bouchard's GPS and track his movements? Let's add another pin in the case against him and prove he was at the motel on the day of the attack."

"Consider it done." Cole climbed to his feet and headed into his office.

Tristan leaned back in his chair. "So we're going to arrest him or bring him in for questioning? He should be at work right now. Should we wait until he's home, or at least not surrounded by the TPD?"

Maddox balled up his napkin and shot it across the room. "As much as I think it sounds like fun to march him through TPD, I think it would be a big fucking headache. My vote is to wait outside his house and pounce when he gets home tonight."

Vic nodded in agreement. "Let's not make a scene. Home is best." He stood up and stretched. "Maddox, I need you to go down and process the two perps. They're going before a judge this afternoon. I doubt they'll get bail, but to be safe, I don't want Tristan anywhere in their vicinity."

Maddox nodded and left the pod.

"Thanks for breakfast. Good work, you guys," Vic called as he followed after Maddox.

Tristan watched his partner leave and then turned to face the few people still sitting at the table, watching him with amused expressions. "What are you laughing about?"

Reed smirked. "You and Maddox, of course."

"What? Why?" Tristan frowned. "I don't get it."

"Jasmina and I were talking about it yesterday," Kiely replied as she stood up and grabbed some of the garbage on the table. "He's been different since you came around. It's a good thing, don't worry."

"Yeah, sure." Tristan groaned as he covered his face with his hands. "He loves to embarrass me and make innuendos in front of Vic. He assures me that it's cool and that Vic knows it's not real."

"That's what I mean." Reed nodded. "That's not normal here at work. He's always so practical and focused."

Tristan laughed sarcastically, "Yeah, in between seducing half the office, you mean."

Jasmina, Kiely and Reed exchanged questioning looks before turning to face him and shaking their heads, "No, he's never slept with anyone he works with that we know of." Kiely said as the other two nodded in agreement.

"Before you came along, I don't think I'd ever even heard him laugh." Jasmina shrugged. "You're good for him, that's all we're saying."

Tristan nodded absently as he stood and headed back to his office, lost in thought. He might be good for Maddox, but Maddox was not good for his heart, that was for sure.

Cole came rushing into the office with a big smile. "He's at home right now if you guys want to grab him. I just pulled up his records, saw that and came to tell you. I still have to look back to the date in question, but thought maybe you'd want to know so you can get a move on him."

Tristan smiled as he jumped to his feet. "Thanks, man." He called as he raced out of the room to track Maddox down. He couldn't wait to see Bouchard's face when they showed up to bring him in for questioning.

CHAPTER
Twenty~Four

MADDOX CLOSED the door to the transport van. There was no way a judge was going to let them out. With luck, they'd put them in jail and throw away the key.

Tristan rushed out the door. "You aren't going to believe this. Cole pulled his GPS, and he's home right now."

Maddox smiled. "Let's get Vic and go get this guy."

He pulled out his phone and called Vic. "Time to roll. We're going to get Bouchard. Let's go."

Tristan shook his head as Maddox hung up. "You do know he's the boss, right?"

Maddox shrugged and took off for the parking

lot. It was rare to arrest a human so high up. He shouldn't be as excited as he was.

Tristan jumped into the passenger seat. They waited by the exit for Vic and several agents in tactical gear to jump in a van and pull up behind them.

Maddox gunned the engine as he followed the GPS to the house.

They pulled up and noticed the Chief's official car in the drive behind his personal car that was at the motel and a blue minivan. His records showed he lived alone, so he hoped there wasn't going to be another human there to get in the way.

Vic led the way, with Maddox and Tristan behind him and the rest of the agents circling the house.

He pounded on the front door and called out their agency name. After a second, Bouchard opened the door, his face red with rage. "What is the meaning of this?" He glanced past Vic and saw Tristan. His face paled.

Vic cleared his throat getting the human's attention. "We'd like to bring you to our office for questioning regarding an attack that happened on April tenth."

"I'm the Chief of Police. You can't just barge in

and demand shit," Bouchard argued as he shifted so he was in Vic's face. "You want to talk to me, go through the proper channels, and don't think I won't have a lawyer with me."

Vic smirked. "You forget we're not part of your human agency. You are wanted for questioning in the attack on a Federal Paranormal Agent. That means we can and will bring you in when and if we feel it's warranted."

"What's going on out here?" A woman came out of a back room with tears running down her face.

Maddox shifted so he could face the woman and take her in fully. Damn it, another human. "Ma'am, I need you to stay back. We need to bring Mr. Bouchard down to the agency to talk to him."

"James?" she questioned as she wiped her face. "What's going on? Why are they taking you?"

"Shelly, it's just a misunderstanding." He pulled her into his arms and gave her a gentle squeeze. "Stay with Brittany and keep her calm. I'll get this straightened out and join you as soon as I can."

He waited until she'd gone back down the hallway before turning to face them once again. "Fine, I'll come in and talk, but I'm taking my own car. I need to be here for my sister and niece. This better be quick."

Vic cocked an eyebrow. "You seem to think you have any right to dictate how this goes. That's not the case. You'll come with us and you'll stay until we get the answers we require." He reached out and grabbed the Chief by the arm. "We've got your ride outside and waiting already."

Maddox and Tristan stepped back to let Vic walk Bouchard down the sidewalk. "Let's go tell the sister what's happening."

They knocked on the open door, Maddox called out. "Hello, ma'am."

After a few seconds of silence, they headed for the door she disappeared into. A soft beep echoed down the hall.

Maddox froze in the doorway. The room had been converted with a hospital bed in the center with a tiny girl on oxygen. The heart monitor next to her showed her heart slowly beating in the 50's.

Shelly spun around with tears running down her face. She rushed over to them and whispered. "Where's James?"

Maddox was at a loss for words. He couldn't stop staring at the little girl who looked like she was out of time.

"He's on his way to the station to answer some

questions," Tristan explained softly as he glanced at the child in the bed.

"I need him here. Brittany doesn't have much time and I can't be alone when it happens." Sobs wracked her body.

Maddox blinked away tears. It was his nature to help, but this girl had no chance of survival. If they did decide to arrest Bouchard, could they wait and do it after the girl passed? That would be the compassionate way to do it. "We'll talk to our boss and see what we can do."

Tristan cleared his throat, "Can I ask you ..."

Shelly nodded. "She's asleep at the moment, so we can talk here if you want. I don't want to leave her."

"I understand." Tristan bit his lip as he glanced at Maddox and then tried again. "We just heard of ... this genetic mutation..."

"It's very rare and very deadly. We knew from birth she had the abnormal gene. They couldn't tell us how long we'd have. We spent years searching for any help we could find. Research studies are limited, and support groups are only online. We've basically been alone. James has been my lifeline through this whole thing."

"When did she start getting sick?"

"About six months ago, we first started seeing the signs it had begun. She went from a vivacious six-year-old to barely being able to walk across a room. She was so tired, out of breath, and then the pain began. Do you know how hard it is to sit and watch your baby slowly waste away without being able to do anything to help fix her or even ease the pain?" Shelly closed her eyes and wiped the tears that fell freely down her face. "She keeps telling me that she'll be okay, that I need to be brave."

Maddox thanked god Tristan was there. He had no words. He wanted to hug the woman and then the girl, but knew he couldn't. The paranormal world didn't have these afflictions, so watching a child suffer was all new to him.

Tristan placed his hand on her shoulder and gave a gentle squeeze. "She sounds like one hell of a kid."

Shelly smiled. "She is. I know I have to say goodbye and it'll be sooner than I'd ever hoped for, but I'm still not ready... I'll never be."

Maddox swallowed loudly. "We'll do everything we can to get your brother back here as soon as possible." Tristan's head spun toward him. "We're sorry for bothering you."

They nodded and left quickly. He needed to be

out of there. On the front porch, he bent over and took deep breaths. "How did you stand being human, that is bullshit."

Tristan shrugged. "It's just something you have to learn to deal with, I guess. It's not something we could avoid. I learned that listening to them and letting them talk can help them cope with it a bit better, you know. It gives them comfort to know that somebody else cares, even if it's a bit hollow."

"You make fun of me for being too helpful now. Just wait, I'm going to find some charities that will let me help. I'm not sure with what exactly, but I don't know how I'll sleep after seeing that."

"You just have to stop, man. You can't let it get to you." Tristan sighed and tentatively reached out, "Can I hug you? It won't help them, but it always makes me feel better and maybe it will for you, too."

Maddox thought a hug sounded amazing. He couldn't remember the last time he'd had a genuine hug from someone. "I'd be open to it."

Tristan laughed as he pulled Maddox into his arms for a massive bear hug. "It's amazing how much this can heal." He whispered into his ear. He held on for a few minutes. "You know you have to step back sometimes. You can't save everyone. You're only one man, an amazing, caring man, but still only one person."

"I don't think I can stop." He mumbled with his mouth pressed against Tristan's shoulder. He pulled back and shook off his mood.

"Then let me help," Tristan said with a soft smile. "Even Batman has someone to help him."

"So, does that make you Robin or Alfred?"

"Robin for sure," Tristan smirked, "Alfred's old and have you seen Robin in spandex.... yummy."

"I hope you're the Chris O'Donnell version more than the Joseph Gordon-Levitt version." He chuckled as he made his way back to Scarlet.

Tristan laughed, "Oh without a doubt, but which Batman would that make you?"

"That would make me George Clooney, but the best Batman was Michael Keaton. Now get in my Batmobile so we can get to the office."

Maddox growled in frustration as they entered the pod. The entire ride back was spent arguing over who played the best batman, superman, and spider-man. They most definitely hadn't agreed on all of them.

Cole poked his head out of his office. "Hey guys, I got something."

They strode in and sat in the empty chairs along the wall.

He handed them each a printout. "This is everywhere Bouchard went over the last three weeks."

"Most of these places look like the usual, but where's this place?" Tristan pointed to a spot on the map. "What's there?"

Cole glanced over his shoulder. "Yeah, notice how many times he's been there? It's an industrial park by the port. I searched property records. It's been in foreclosure for a decade."

Tristan frowned. "Who owns it?"

"Some bottling company that went out of business years ago."

"So we have no idea why he'd be going there since it's supposed to be abandoned?" Tristan frowned.

Maddox folded the paper. "I think we should go check it out before we talk to Bouchard."

Tristan shrugged. "Sounds good. Let's go."

Maddox plugged the address into Scarlet's GPS.

Ten minutes later, they pulled into the empty parking lot across the street from the building. "It doesn't look like anyone's been here for years. What would he be doing down here?"

The whole area looked like the land that time forgot. "Hell, I don't even see any street people and that's not normal. Most places like this are a bit of a haven for them. Do you know anyone at the electric company who can check if the electricity is still on? It may give us an idea of what's going on in there."

Maddox's phone vibrated in the cupholder. "It's Jaylen." He put the call on speaker. "Hey Jaylen, what's up?"

"We just got the call that another kid's been taken. It was a ten-year-old Caucasian girl taken from the Museum of Science and Industry. She was there on a field trip. She has black hair and green eyes."

Maddox cursed as he punched the steering wheel. "It's too soon. We were supposed to have another day or two before the pattern repeated."

Tristan scowled, "Why did they change their routine now? This doesn't make sense."

"They have the whole area shut down and all available units searching the area. I heard the teacher is devastated." Jaylen continued.

"Thanks, keep us posted if you can." Tristan sighed as he faced Maddox as the other man hit the end button on the phone. "That means tomorrow a paranormal 10-year-old girl is going to go missing."

"I have never had a case with so few leads. I feel so useless and it's really pissing me off." Maddox growled as he threw his head back against the seat.

They lapsed into silence as they took a minute to absorb the ramifications of the call. Tristan suddenly sat up straighter and smacked Maddox absently, "Look."

Maddox cocked his head, "What the hell?"

"That is what we call a kidnapper van," Tristan mumbled as he stared intently at the vehicle pulling up in front of the warehouse.

It pulled in between two buildings and stopped next to a door all the way in the back. Two men got out and went around the back of the van.

Maddox sat forward. "What the actual fuck!"

He was stunned as he watched them pull a girl with black hair out of the back. She was fighting them but couldn't get free. He opened his door to run after them, but Tristan pulled him back.

"We need to call this in and get back-up. This has to be where they've been taking the kids and how the hell is Bouchard involved in this?"

Maddox grabbed his phone and slammed his fingers on the screen as he dialed Vic. "Cole gave us an address to check out for Bouchard. We got a call that another human kid had been taken. A van just pulled up to the building we're watching, and a girl was forcibly taken inside. We need everyone you can spare. Bring them all. We need to get in there and save these kids."

"Calm down, I'll get the team assembled and we'll head out. Just sit tight and keep an eye out. We'll get there as quickly as we can." Vic assured him before hanging up.

Maddox ended the call and tossed the phone on the dashboard. "I'm so scared to go in there. The chance that all the kids are in there is slim. They've likely been trafficked."

"Maybe, but that doesn't mean we can't save her and get information on the rest. Shutting this operation down will be a huge win for all the kids they would've taken in the future. We've got to keep in mind all the good with the bad." Tristan frowned as he watched the building. "And maybe we'll get a miracle and we'll find them all safe and healthy. You have to have hope, man."

The wait for Vic and the cavalry to get there was painful. Maddox itched to storm inside and beat the two men to a bloody pulp.

Finally, his phone rang. "Vic, how long?"

"We're pulling up now. You should see a chopper any second, and we've got some boats in the water. There's no way these guys can get away."

A few moments later, the P.I.S. vans pulled up without their sirens. Maddox moved to the front of the line and drove straight for the van, stopping his car in front of theirs. Vic's vehicle and another van blocked the other two sides.

Maddox jumped out of the Scarlet, his wings already out.

Tristan chased after him and stopped beside him to whisper in his ear, "Um, is this a bad time to ask you to slap my ass so my wings will come out too?"

Maddox blinked at him for a second, trying to comprehend what he was asking, then he wound up and slapped as hard as he could.

"This really isn't the time for your kinky shit, guys. Get your heads in the game, and I mean the ones on your damn shoulders." Vic growled as he walked up to them.

Tristan groaned as he felt his wings pop out. "Sorry, sir. I don't know how to control them yet and I know this worked last time. I just wanted to be prepared."

Vic rolled his eyes. "You two are going to be the death of me."

They lined up behind the tactical team and followed as they counted down and rammed the doors open.

Maddox gave a second for his eyes to adjust. Shouts could be heard from every corner as several people were running for the exits. Maddox didn't chase after any. He left them to the other agents and followed the sound of several beeping machines. Large sheets of plastic were hung in the center, creating a rectangle. Their team closed in from every angle and tore through the sheets at the same time.

Tristan stumbled to a stop, "Holy fucking shit!" He mumbled as his head swiveled back and forth, taking in the small area.

Ten hospital beds were set up in a circle. Every kid they'd been searching for was hooked up to machines. "This is not what I was expecting." Maddox shook his head in shock.

He ran up to the closest bed and shook the boy in the bed. He moaned quietly, but couldn't open his eyes. "I think they're being sedated."

"As soon as the place is secure, I'll have Dr. Obinski come in and check the kids out," Tristan called out as he typed on his phone.

Maddox pulled out his phone and called Jaylen. "You aren't going to believe this. We found all nine kids, including the girl taken this morning. I'll text you the address. The kids are all sedated and hooked to machines. We have a paranormal doctor coming in. Vic's going to reach out to TPD officially, but we thought you deserved to know." He hung up and walked over to Vic and Tristan.

Vic held up a hand to get the group's attention. "Everyone take a bed and search everywhere. Check every label, if there's any paperwork scour it for any clues as to what they've been doing to these kids. Don't touch the actual kids or IV's. We need the medical team to handle it."

Maddox went back to the boy's bed and searched through the drawers of the cabinet next to him. If they'd been documenting what they were doing to the kids, it wasn't on physical paper.

Tristan was next to the girl they'd brought in that morning. She was sedated, but it looked like they interrupted them before they could hook her up to anything.

Tristan looked up with a smile. "Sounds like we have company. Dr. Obinski should be with them."

A moment later, the doctor came running in with his bag in hand and a couple of doctors following behind him. "I brought some help since I wasn't sure what we'd find." He called out as they moved up to stand beside them. "This is Dr. Jed Kingston and Dr. Reed McLeod."

Tristan stepped back and let the doctors do their thing. He turned to Maddox, "What in the fuck was Bouchard doing here with these kids?"

"I have my theories. Vic and Obinski have this handled. We'll just get in the way. Let's go see what your guy has to say."

They used the lights and sirens and got back to the office in minutes. Maddox wasn't sure which of them was angrier as they stormed down the hall and into the holding area. He pointed at the agent at the desk. "Get James Bouchard in room two now." Maddox couldn't wait to get his hands on the prick and find out what he was doing with the kids.

CHAPTER
Twenty-Five

TRISTAN CROSSED his arms and leaned against the wall as he studied the man sitting at the table. He was struggling to come to terms with the fact that this man, the Chief of the department, was also the one kidnapping kids.

"Are you ready to explain why you brought me down here and locked me in a cell? I believe with the position I hold, I deserved a bit more respect than that." Chief Bouchard announced in a haughty tone.

Tristan shook his head, "You were right where you belong, you piece of shit. Do you want to know where we just came from? What we just saw and can link you to?"

Bouchard's face turned red. He became so angry at Tristan's words. "You can't speak to me that way."

Maddox smirked from his place next to Tristan, "Does the address 2420 Gordon Street mean anything to you?"

Tristan moved forward and sat across from the other man. "That look," Tristan grinned and pointed at Bouchard as his face went deathly white. "tells me you know exactly what we're referring to. It's time to talk and see if you can get yourself out of this mess you've created. We've got you for nine counts of abduction of a minor, two counts of conspiracy to impede or injure an officer. Yeah, we know you're the one behind the attack on me at the motel."

Maddox crossed his arms as he studied the older man. "We still have to add counts for the original attack on you that caused your transformation."

Tristan glanced up at his partner in shock before recovering and turning back to Bouchard to see his response.

"I believe it's time I called in my lawyer," James said as he leaned back in his chair and stared at the wall behind them.

Maddox shrugged. "Don't worry, we'll explain to Shelly and Brittany why you aren't coming home tonight." He pushed off the wall and walked behind Bouchard. "We saw her, you know. Laying in that hospital bed. Why would you do anything to risk your freedom when you know you don't have much time left with her?"

"You know nothing about any of it. Everything I've done, I did for her. She's a child and deserves a chance at life. Don't speak of her, you bastard." Bouchard screamed as he pounded on the table. He slumped back in his chair as his tears began to fall. "I just wanted to help her."

Tristan sighed. "Look, we can make arrangements for you to be with her. You can say goodbye and be there for your sister. But you need to work with us, explain what we found, and give us a reason to help you."

Bouchard leaned forward eagerly. "You'd let me go home to be with them and wait to arrest me?"

Maddox stopped next to Tristan. "We'd station an agent outside your home and they'd follow you anywhere you went to make sure you didn't flee, but I think we can give you that. You just have to tell us everything you've done."

"What do you want to know first?" Bouchard asked with a resigned sigh. "I'll tell you anything you want to know if it means I can be with them till the end."

Tristan blew out a breath as he nodded to

Maddox, "Start at the beginning, and don't leave anything out."

Bouchard licked his lips. "Over the years, we'd searched the world for anything that could fix the broken gene in Brittany, but nothing ever worked out. Every trial failed, every hope was destroyed. Then six months ago she developed her first symptom, and we knew it was the beginning of the end. Shelly came to me, devastated. Our time was up. At first, I redoubled my efforts, but I soon realized it was for naught."

James looked up to Tristan with pleading in his eyes, "I never meant to hurt anyone, and I swear the kids were looked after and never harmed. I just need to find a way to save my baby girl."

"How do the kids fit into this, though? I don't understand." Tristan demanded.

"Human kids have the gene, but only a handful are abnormal, right?" Bouchard explained as he looked between the two of them. "It's a paranormal gene, so I thought what if we used paranormal genes to fix the bad ones?"

Tristan cursed as he stood up and paced the small confines of the interrogation room. "None of the human kids have the abnormality though, so why did you think they'd be of use to you?"

"I was desperate. I found some scientists on the dark web who, for a price, agreed to help me study the kid's genetic makeup to see if we could find similarities and their differences in the hopes it would bring us a step closer." He shook his head and shrugged. "It was a failure. Nothing we did worked."

"How does Tristan fit into all of this?" Maddox growled softly.

"He was too damn good at his job. He was getting too close and I couldn't let him stop my chances of saving Brittany. I hired some lowlifes from the docks to take him out. I didn't know it would change him like that, though."

Tristan froze as he looked up in surprise and shock. "Fucking hell."

"And the motel?" Maddox prompted.

"I thought maybe if he could come back from the dead, that it might have been the missing piece I needed to save her. So, I hired those two goons to kidnap him and bring him to the lab for testing. I didn't count on you being there to help him."

"What did you do to the kids?" Tristan demanded as he leaned over the table glaring at his old Chief.

"Beyond taking blood, I didn't do anything. You'd have to talk to the scientists to get more specifics. I think we took samples of stuff, but I really don't know."

Maddox tapped Tristan on the shoulder. "I think we got enough." He turned back to Bouchard. "Give us a few to run this up the chain, but we'll get someone in here to take you home and like we said, someone will be with you twenty-four seven. When your niece has passed, you'll come back in here and write up your confession for all of the crimes."

Bouchard nodded, but didn't say anything.

Tristan followed Maddox out of the room. As soon as the door closed, Tristan turned to his partner. "Do you really think they'll allow him to go like that? He abducted nine kids, wouldn't the parents freak out if they found out he was free?"

Maddox shrugged. "I have no idea, but I saw that kid and her mom and I offered it because of them, not for him. Either way, it's not our decision. We'll run it by Vic and let him make the decision." He pulled his phone out of his pocket. "Just got a text. Obinski moved all the paranormal kids to Shifter General. Want to head over there?"

Tristan nodded and headed down the hall. So much had happened in a very short time, and he felt a bit adrift. Only the company of his partner, the steadfast asshole that he was, kept him from losing his shit.

"How did you know about the attack that turned me?" He asked Maddox as they made their way outside of the building.

Maddox snorted. "Ha, I didn't really believe it, but thought I would throw it out there and see how he responded. I honestly did not expect him to admit to it."

"You had me fooled. I was sure you knew something I didn't." Tristan pulled the door open to Scarlet and paused. "Any chance you're going to let me drive her yet?"

"You'll have to buy me dinner, fuck me hard, and buy me breakfast, and maybe I'll consider it." He smirked as he climbed into the car.

Tristan gaped at him, "What the fuck?" He laughed, "I swear to God I never know what will come out of your mouth from one minute to the next. But I did hear that you don't screw your coworkers, despite what you may have said last night."

Maddox gunned the engine as they pulled out onto the street. "Haven't you figured out by now that you can't believe half the shit I say? If I had a therapist, they would probably say it's a defense mechanism."

"That might be half the problem, don't you think? I don't know where I stand with you because I can never believe a damn thing you say." Tristan let his head fall back on the headrest. "You're exhausting to deal with sometimes."

Maddox skidded the car to a stop, then pulled over. His fingers tapped the steering wheel for a few seconds before he turned and grabbed Tristan by the back of the neck and made him look at him. "No lies, no bullshit. This is me telling you the truth. I've never met anyone like you. Everything I thought I wanted in life is bullshit since I met you. You make me crazy, my skin itches when you're nearby. I haven't ever messed with a co-worker, so teasing you and keeping you at arm's length was the best I could do."

Tristan sputtered in shock as he studied Maddox's eyes for the truth of his words. "Just one question." He licked his lips. "Your skin itches in a good way, right?"

Maddox gave him a dimpled smile. "To you, it's a good thing. For me, it sucks. It itches because I want to touch you and mark you and make you mine. I'm doing everything I can to not cross any lines, but your scent makes that impossible." He pulled him close and paused when they were an inch apart.

Was he giving Tristan one last chance to protest?

Maddox pressed his mouth gently against Tristan's. He turned his head and deepened the kiss until they were moaning.

Tristan pulled back and licked his lips, tasting Maddox there, "I.." he shuddered as a wave of desire swept through him and he laughed. "I so did not expect that in a million years."

"I think it's part my patience running out and part seriously fucked up emotional day. I'm sorry if you didn't want that. I know I should have asked." He turned back and pulled out onto the road.

"I didn't say that. I was surprised, that's all." Tristan grinned. "Maybe next time we can do it someplace not in the car. It was fun as teenagers, but I want to touch you and the console is in my way."

"That might be a good thing. If we start, I don't think I can stop and we need to get to the hospital." He stared straight ahead, his face serious again.

They lapsed into silence as they made the rest of the trip to the hospital. They pulled into the parking lot of the six-story hospital and found a spot.

"Did he say where he took them?" Tristan asked as he climbed out of the car.

Maddox checked his phone. "No, but I'll text him and let him know we're here. Maybe he can meet us in the lobby or something."

"Should we go to the ER or the main entrance?" Tristan glanced between the two entrances. "I'd think they'd have come in as an emergency and then been taken someplace, right?"

Maddox stared at his phone, then nodded. "Yeah, he says go through the main entrance and take the elevator to the fifth-floor pediatric unit. We should see a closed- off section with agents guarding the area."

They headed into the hospital and asked one of the volunteers for directions to the elevator. They stayed silent as they made their way to the floor. As the doors opened, they glanced in both directions before seeing an agent standing down to the left. They flashed their IDs to the guard and went inside. Dr. Obinski looked up as they entered and waved them over.

"Hey, guys." He greeted them with a tired sigh. "Good news. The kids seem to be in good condition. We're still running tests, but so far, everything seems positive."

Maddox nodded. "That's good to hear. Bouchard admitted he arranged everything. He was trying to save his niece and said he was out of options. I gotta tell you, we saw the niece this morning. If she lives through the weekend, it'll be a miracle."

Obinski shook his head. "That is unfortunate. After our discussion, I did some research and there really hasn't been any promising studies."

"It gets better. After my transformation, he tried to have me taken. He had a theory that since I was human and turned that maybe my blood could save her." Tristan shook his head and shrugged in a can you believe it kind of way.

Obinski scratched his chin. "Interesting. I don't think I read anything where they tried a human turned paranormal subject. Your agents caught the doctors that were running this. If I talk to them and see their methods, maybe I can try to help her. You'd have to be willing Tristan, and the mom would have to agree too. Given the girl is almost out of time, she may agree that they have nothing to lose."

Tristan frowned as he thought it over. "What would the risks involved be for me and the kid?"

Dr. Obinski hesitated and then said. "I'm not sure if this is the exact same protocol, but in circumstances where we've done gene therapy, we'd take a lot of your blood and send it to the lab to isolate the paranormal genes. From there, they will pull out the proteins and put them in a therapeutic working gene that will be delivered via IV infusion to the child. For you Tristan, there really isn't any risk at all."

"And Brittany?" Maddox questioned.

"She could reject it, have an inflammatory response, and even die. But if this is her last chance, then I think it's worth a try. From start to finish, the process takes about forty-eight hours. We need to convince the mother and get the kid in here as quickly as possible."

Maddox pulled his phone out of his pocket. "I'll update Vic and get approval for them to bring Bouchard here if the mom agrees." He glanced up at Tristan. "You and I need to get to their house and convince her."

"I'll drive while you make the calls." Tristan winked as he pushed past Maddox.

"One kiss is not the same as what my conditions were, but since this is for a kid, I'll agree this one time. But if Scarlet rejects you and stalls out or something, don't blame me. I don't even know how well you can handle such a powerful woman." He tossed him the keys as they got on the elevator.

Tristan laughed as he caught the keys and smirked. "Admit it, that kiss was out of this world and that's why you're agreeing, isn't it?"

"Ha! Your ego's getting out of control. Wait until you've had sex with a paranormal, that is truly out of this world. You probably need to take a day or two off after to recuperate the first few times."

"So, I guess that means sex with myself doesn't count?" Tristan called out as they stepped off the elevator. "And what should I tell Vic about why I'm not at work? He said no calling out for kinky shit, remember."

"First of all, was the solo sex done at my condo, in my shower? Second, you can tell Vic it's a cold. He'll know you are full of shit because we don't get colds, but legally, he can't stop you."

"A gentleman doesn't kiss and tell, or I guess in this case, stroke and tell." Tristan winked at him.

"I was about to say if you kissed yourself, I would pay to see that!" Maddox tossed over his shoulder as he walked to the passenger side of Scarlet. "In all seriousness though, I did see a cat shifter once give himself a blow job. I never knew they were so freaking flexible."

"Let me guess. You took him to the bathroom to put that flexibility to the test, didn't you?"

"If I'd met him in a bar, I probably would have, but in this case, we were arresting him for exposing himself at a dog park."

"And you guys say humans are weird. Every time you tell me a story, I think nope, they can't top that, and then you do."

He quirked an eyebrow at him. "Didn't you guys have that singer who removed a rib so he could suck himself?"

"Well shit, I always thought he wasn't human." Tristan shrugged. "Guess neither side wants to claim him."

Their idle banter died as they made their way back to James Bouchard's house to see Shelly and try to convince her that this might be her only chance. Tristan pulled up at the curb outside the house and turned Scarlet off. "Thanks, baby." He whispered as he patted the dashboard with a loving touch.

Maddox shook his head. "I feel dirty just watching you with her." He muttered as he climbed out.

Tristan laughed as he followed Maddox up to the door. He knocked, and they waited patiently as the seconds ticked by without Shelly answering the door.

"Do you think something happened and she left?" Tristan asked softly.

Before Maddox could reply, the door opened and

Shelly peeked out at them with her red-rimmed eyes. "What do you guys want now?"

"If you don't mind letting us inside, we'd like to talk to you," Maddox asked.

She nodded and pulled the door open. "Sure, but let's go back to Brittany's room."

They followed her down the hall. Tristan's heart sank seeing her heart rate was now in the forties.

Maddox stood by the window. "This may be hard for you to hear, but your brother is under arrest. He had nine children kidnapped and was holding them in a warehouse where they were running tests on them. Not that it makes it right, but he was trying to find a cure for your daughter."

Shelly's hands came up to cover her mouth as she shook her head back and forth in shock. "No, he wouldn't do that. He couldn't do that." She cried as her tears began to flow for a different reason now.

"He confessed to everything, and the children are all in hospitals now being reunited with their families."

She shook her head. "Nine other mothers were going through the worst pain imaginable, all in the hopes of saving mine. I don't know that I can forgive him for that."

"Ma'am," Tristan stepped forward and offered

her a tissue from the box he found on the table beside the bed. "I know what he did was wrong, and I don't condone it in any way. But he might have been onto something and that's why we're here."

Shelly wiped her eyes. "What do you mean? I don't understand."

"Almost two weeks ago, I was human. I was attacked, and my body transformed me and brought me back from death. Your brother thinks my DNA can repair your daughter's genes. It's a long shot, but to be frank, she doesn't have much time left. This could be your last chance."

"What does that mean, exactly?"

"One of the doctors who treated me during my change thinks they can do gene therapy and introduce my paranormal gene into your daughter and let it heal her broken one. The process will take a bit, so we have to get started right away. Your daughter doesn't have much longer. Come to the hospital with us and Dr. Obinski can explain the process. But there is one thing you have to know upfront before we go any farther."

"And that is?"

Tristan glanced at Maddox for reassurance before looking back into Shelly's eyes. "If it works, there is a chance she could become paranormal like I did."

She walked over to the bed and stared down at Brittany. "So, my choices are sit here and watch her waste away, let you try the experiment and it kills her, or let you try and it heals her, but she may become paranormal..."

Maddox and Tristan stood silently, letting her weigh her options.

Finally, she turned and nodded at them. "Let's do it. Let's try the experiment. I couldn't care less if she changes. At least I'll have her, but not trying is a guaranteed death sentence."

Maddox grabbed his phone and dialed Obinski. "They've agreed to the therapy. I'll text you the address. Can you send over an ambulance to transport her?"

Tristan watched him, wishing the phone had been on speaker.

"Sounds good. See you in a few." He slid his phone back into his pocket. "We'll stay with her while you go pack a bag. I expect you'll be at the hospital for a few days."

She gave them a hopeful smile as she raced out of the room.

"I swear to god if we kill this girl, I don't know

how I'll live with myself," Maddox growled as he stared down at her.

Tristan moved to stand beside him and placed a hand on his shoulder. "You can't look at it like that. No matter what happens, we gave her a chance. Death is standing in the room waiting to guide her to her afterlife."

Maddox leaned back and stared around the room. "Are you being facetious, or can you really see a grim reaper? I didn't know supes could see them."

Tristan huffed out a laugh at the panic on Maddox's face. "No, I can't see them, but that doesn't mean they aren't here. I just meant that her time is almost up. We're not causing her death, but we might cause her to live."

A knock on the front door broke the tension. "That must be the ambulance. I'll go let them in."

Maddox waited until Tristan left the room before he too glanced around the room. "If you're here, please give us as much time as you can. Let us see if this works, don't take her too soon."

He stepped away from the bed as the EMTs walked in, pulling a stretcher. They nodded to him and then prepared Brittany for transport. Within a minute, they had the small child on the bed, strapped down, and were ready to head back outside. Tristan followed behind them solemnly. No matter what he said, he knew he'd lied to Maddox. He'd always carry the guilt if this didn't work, but that wasn't going to make him not try.

Maddox was standing next to the door with Shelly. "You can ride in the ambulance and we'll be right behind you guys."

They followed them out to the ambulance and waited for them to get her settled. Maddox glanced over at Tristan. "Since you are being the hero here and possibly saving her, it's only fair you get to drive Scarlet to the hospital. It's the least I can do."

Tristan swallowed past the lump in his throat and gave Maddox a small smile. "Either way, this isn't going to kill me. I'm not the hero of this story. It's all that little girl in there fighting for her life."

He climbed into Scarlet and turned her on. The rev of the engine sent chills down his spine. "She just may be the only woman I could love." He winked at Maddox as he climbed into the car.

"My mom and Tallie might be upset by that fact. Hell, what about your mom?"

"A mom's love is very different." Tristan grinned, "But yeah, don't tell Tallie on me. I don't need a hormonal teenager getting pissed at me."

"Speaking of your mom, would you want her

here? I know you don't think there's much risk, but you never know."

"Nah," Tristan shook his head, "She wouldn't understand what was going on anyway. Her good days are few and far between anymore. Besides, I'm just giving some blood. That's pretty routine anymore."

The rest of the ride was silent as they followed the ambulance back to Shifter General. Dr. Obinski was standing by the doors, ready for them.

Tristan found a parking spot and rushed to catch up with them. They were led back to the same wing the other kids were being sequestered in, but there was a lot more activity this time. They'd started letting the parents in to see the kids.

As Tristan and Maddox walked down the hall, several people stepped out of their rooms and thanked them. They were pulled in for hugs and several people shook their hands.

Dr. Obinski glanced back at them. "I may have let it slip you were the two who found all nine children."

Tristan glared at the doctor. "Thanks for that."

It wasn't that he minded the thanks and hugs, but he felt almost guilty for receiving them. He didn't find those kids for the gratitude. And part of him hated that because Bouchard had taken them. They might have discovered a way to save thousands of lives. These kids weren't hurt, but it still felt like that ethical question they asked him in the academy once. Do you sacrifice one to save many? When you asked that in relation to kids, it became even harder to answer.

He smiled and accepted the hugs, but inside each one was a lash against his heart until finally, they made it past the parents and into a quiet room.

Dr. Obinski popped his head in. "We're getting Brittany comfortable now. The lab techs are on their way up to get your blood." He started to leave, then glanced back. "Smile, even if this doesn't work, you still opened up a whole new avenue of research that may lead to saving the next person."

When they were alone, Maddox sat down next to him. "Do you want me to hold your hand while they stick you?"

Tristan cocked one eyebrow and studied Maddox, "I feel like no matter how I answer that, it'll be the wrong one. It's a trick question, isn't it?"

The lab tech entered the room and smiled at the two of them. "This won't take but a few minutes." She inspected each of his arms until she found a good vein and nodded. "Put your arm up here and make a fist, while I insert the needle."

Tristan watched intently as the tech took vile after vile of blood. "Are you taking all of it?"

The tech laughed. "Not even close. This is actually less than we'd take if you gave blood at a donation center. But if you're feeling queasy or faint, let me know and we can get you a soda and some crackers."

Tristan frowned, "I'm fine."

The Tech winked at him as she applied the bandage and cleaned up. "You're all done."

"I think he would feel a lot better if you had a lollipop or a sticker?" Maddox said innocently.

Tristan rolled his eyes as the tech laughed. A few minutes later, they walked out of the lab with Tristan sucking on his lollipop and a smile on his face.

CHAPTER
Twenty~Six

VIC WAVED THEM OVER. "Jaylen is here with the Deputy Chief of police and the detectives in charge of the human cases. They want a debriefing of what happened. I don't think they know yet the Chief is involved. I got the impression from Jaylen they don't know why they can't get a hold of him."

Maddox snorted. "I can't wait to see their faces when we tell them we arrested him."

Vic nodded. "They have closed off the break room down the hall for us to talk privately."

The trio made their way to the room and shook hands with Jaylen, who was standing just outside the door.

"I can't believe you guys cracked the case and saved all nine kids."

Vic patted him on the back. "Let's go make sure they know how valuable you were to us."

A balding man in his fifties stood up and shook hands with each of them. Maddox was impressed. He expected them to be condescending and uncomfortable. "I'm Deputy Chief Barlowe and these are Detectives Patterson and Davies, who were the leads on the cases from our side. Can you give us a rundown of how this all came down, because, to be honest, we didn't even know about your cases?" He glanced at Jaylen as he sat back down.

Maddox shook hands with each, then sat down. "We had four kids missing at the time Tristan was attacked and joined the dark side. He remembered that you guys had missing kids too and after a lot of attempts to get the files from you guys, we went to Jaylen and asked him to help."

Tristan nodded. "If it wasn't for him, we never would have been able to see the connections. What we didn't expect to find out is that your Chief Bouchard was behind all of it and we have him in custody at our offices."

Barlowe slammed his hand on the table. "Excuse me? You arrested him as a suspect?"

Tristan smiled. "We were looking into him on an unrelated case when we found the connection between him and the warehouse where we found the kids."

Vic tapped his fingers on the table. "Once we have everything documented, we'll send it over, but suffice it to say your guy isn't getting out any time soon."

Patterson cleared his throat. "I don't care who found the kids. I'm just glad you recovered all of them. Are any of yours hurt? Ours are fine, other than traumatized from the ordeal."

"Same with ours. I think they're all going to be fine. Did you know your Chief had a sick niece?"

Barlowe nodded as the other three shook their heads.

Maddox continued. "There may be a silver lining to this case. Bouchard had those kids taken and tested on to try and save his niece, and because of his work and Tristan's attack and transformation, we may have a way to save her."

Jaylen smiled broadly. "I'm sorry for everyone involved, but that's also great news."

Vic pointed at him as he stared down Barlowe. "This kid deserves a promotion, so I hope you take care of him."

Barlowe nodded but didn't say anything.

Vic stood up. "If there's nothing else, we need to

get back to the families. We'll have everything we have sent over as soon as possible."

Maddox opened Bouchard's cell and waved for him to exit. "We're taking you to the hospital."

The older man's face paled. "Is it Brittany?"

Maddox nodded. "Yes, but not like you think. We have a doctor who is trying a procedure on her today. He has high hopes for its success, but just in case we wanted to give you the opportunity to see her one more time before they start."

Tears poured down Bouchard's face. "I know it's more than I deserve, so I thank you."

Tristan shook his head at him. "We're really spoiling you. They'll have Brittany in a pre-op room on a different floor so we won't march you in front of the families. We can't promise one of them wouldn't try to hurt you. You can't imagine how scary a vampire and dragon can be when you've crossed them."

Maddox shouldn't have enjoyed how scared the man looked, but honestly, he deserved that and so much worse.

They loaded him into the transport van. Logan

and his partner Payton sat on either side of him for the duration of the ride.

They'd tried to go in through the least used entrance, but feds showing up with a man in handcuffs tended to get noticed.

Maddox pushed the button for the elevator. "Fuck."

One of the fathers walked in with a coffee in hand. "Is that him? Is that the guy who took my son?"

Tristan rushed forward and held him back. "This isn't the time nor the place. You'll have your chance to face him, but that's not right now. Go be with your son, please."

The man didn't look thrilled, but he nodded and went down the hall to another set of elevators.

The doors finally opened, and the group shuffled on. It was silent as they rode up to the third floor.

Maddox checked his phone as they got out. "We need to go to room 3042."

After a couple of turns, they saw Dr. Obinski and two nurses talking outside of a room. He saw them and hastily finished his conversation with the nurses.

"Everything is all set. The lab finished early this

morning and we're ready to begin as soon as you give the go-ahead."

Maddox turned and took the handcuffs off Bouchard. "Tristan and I are going to be in there with you and Logan and Payton will be outside this door, so don't do anything stupid."

Bouchard nodded solemnly.

Maddox took a deep breath and opened the door. He really didn't want to see the girl again. His breath caught when he saw her. How she looked even smaller than the day before was beyond his understanding. If she lasted the day, he would be shocked.

Bouchard gave Shelly a hug and hushed her sobs. He leaned over the bed. "Lovebug, open your eyes."

Everyone held their breath, waiting to see what would happen.

Amazingly, she managed to open them a crack. "Uncle James, where have you been?"

"I'm sorry honey, I got tied up with work, but I'm here now." His voice cracked on the last word. "I heard the doctors have a magic potion they are going to give you and it's going to make you all better."

Behind him, Shelly hiccupped and turned, collapsing against Tristan. Maddox bit back a laugh at the shocked look on his partner's face before he snapped out of it and hugged her back.

The lump in Maddox's throat was threatening to suffocate him. He couldn't wait to get out of the room.

Bouchard grabbed Brittany's hands and brought them to his face, kissing the top of each one. "As soon as you are out of here, we're going to Disney World and I'm buying you all the princess dresses you could want."

"Can we get mommy one too?" Her tiny voice could barely be heard over the beeping of the heart monitor.

"Absolutely. We'll make sure to get you matching dresses, too." He laughed with her. "I'm going to step out and let the doctors do their work."

She smiled up at him as he walked backward with his eyes locked on her until he reached the door and finally turned to go through it.

Maddox and Tristan followed after him until they all leaned against the wall outside her room.

Five hours later, Maddox walked down the hall with a tray of coffees in his hand. A scream reverberated down the corridor. He ran as fast as he could while trying not to spill the hot liquid. Bouchard stood at the door, trying to get inside, but Logan was holding him back.

Maddox skidded to a stop next to Tristan. "Do we know anything?"

"No, it's been quiet the entire time you were gone. That didn't sound good though, did it?" Tristan asked as he shifted from foot to foot.

"Shit." Maddox wanted to throw up. They knew the chance of the infusion working was slim, but he still had held out hope that it would.

Bouchard sobbed against Logan while everyone waited quietly.

The door finally opened. Dr. Obinski walked out, beaming from ear to ear. "Her heart rate is picking back up, her blood pressure is stabilizing, and the color is coming back to her extremities."

Shelly stepped past him and pulled Bouchard into a hug. "I think it's going to work. I think she's going to live."

Dr. Obinski held his hand up. "Like I said a few minutes ago. This is very promising, but we have to take this one minute at a time. She is literally the first person to ever have this done, so we are in uncharted waters here."

Bouchard turned to Maddox and Tristan. "Can I go inside and see her?"

Payton waited for Maddox to nod. "Logan and I can take him inside so you guys can talk to doc."

Dr. Obinski waited until they were alone, then hunched over with his hands on his knees and let out a deep breath. "This has been one of the scariest days of my professional career. I honestly didn't expect it to work."

Tristan swallowed audibly as he slumped against the wall. "I think I'm in shock. I don't know what to even think at this point."

"I do." Maddox slapped him on the shoulder. "This means they are going to turn you into a pin cushion now. But don't worry, I'll make sure they have lots of lollipops for you."

"Fuck off," Tristan grumbled as he fought not to laugh. "So, what happens next from here?"

"We'll have to create a joint clinical trial with the human scientists. During that time, we'll scour the earth for more people like you, so we aren't sticking you every day. If the trial is successful, we can get emergency approval on a case-by-case basis while the humans get their FDA to give full approval. The overall process is going to take years, but we should start being able to save lives almost immediately." Dr. Obinski replied tiredly.

Tristan nodded slowly as he attempted to

process all that information. "I... uh... okay then. I guess I'll... just wait ..." He shrugged and looked at Maddox helplessly. "I don't even know what I'm saying."

"Look at it this way. You're going to be in the history books now. They might even name this after you. You're a superhero." Maddox squeezed his shoulder affectionately. "Just don't go getting a big head about it or the pod, and I will make sure to take you down a notch."

Maddox held his hand out to Dr. Obinski. "Thank you for doing all of this. I know it was a risk that some doctors may not have been willing to take. We'll let you get back to your patient."

Vic, Cole, and Reed came down the hall. "You guys have been here all day. Why don't you get out of here and we'll worry about getting Bouchard back to his cell? And by getting out of here, I mean go back to the office and start the mountain of paperwork that you have to do. There are a hundred people banging on our doors for details."

Maddox blew out a deep breath. "No rest for two heroes? Not even an afternoon off?"

"Hey, I thought I was the superhero. You trying to take my spotlight already?"

"I did help rescue nine, yes nine, children. That's worth something," he said sarcastically.

Tristan patted him on the shoulder. "We'll be sure to get you some ice cream or a treat on the way home to celebrate."

Vic shook his head. "You two are going to give me an ulcer. Get out of here and go do some work." He sounded grumpy, but Maddox knew he was only joking.

Maddox and Tristan made their way outside. The emotion of the day had been draining. Maddox stopped on the sidewalk. "Well shit, we came in the transport van. How the hell are we getting back to the office?"

Epilogue

MADDOX SAT on his couch sipping a beer. "This has been one hell of a month and it's not even over yet."

Tristan snorted. "you're telling me. On top of all the work stuff, I also changed species, or whatever you would call it."

Maddox tipped his beer at him. "Good point. You win." They lapsed into silence for a minute. "I can't imagine you're going to make the motel your permanent residence. My lease is up soon. What do you think about maybe looking for a two-bedroom place?"

"You want me to be your roommate? You've always lived alone. You sure you're ready to share your space with someone else like that?"

Maddox picked at the label of his bottle. "Truthfully... I like you... like more than as a partner. But you're right, I have been alone for a long time. I thought maybe roommates would be a good step forward, not too much pressure on either of us. And we're adults. If it doesn't work out between us romantically, we can still be roommates, right?"

Tristan hesitated as he took a sip of his beer. "I don't know about that last part, but I'm willing to give it a try. I can't promise anything more than that though. I'm..." He licked his lips and shifted on the couch to face Maddox, "When I care, I'm all in. So, if it didn't work out, I don't know that I could be close to you."

Maddox grabbed Tristan's shirt and pulled him close. "Let me be clear. I am all in, too. I'll stand in the middle of the pod tomorrow and tell everyone that I like you if that proves anything. I just wanted you to have an easy out."

Tristan winced. "Uh, you don't have to go that far just yet." He bit his lip and closed the short distance between them. "But we don't have to keep it a secret either." He pressed their lips together for a sweet kiss before pulling back and smiling, "Because if you're mine, I'll make sure everyone knows it anyway."

The End

Maddox and Tristan are back with a whole new adventure. Buy *Stitched Under Fire*: https://amzn.to/3uUqDeR

Keep reading for a sneak peak of book two - Stitched Under Fire

About the Authors

Cassidy lives in the Tampa, Florida area with her high school sweetheart, their three children, her dog Flynn who she loves obsessively, and her grand dog, Ryder. She loves reading and going to the movies. She also loves to travel and hopes to one day watch a baseball game in every MLB stadium in the country.

She also writes under the pen name C.K. O'Connor. Books by C.K. range from sweet romance to young adult to historical romance.

To learn more about C.K. / Cassidy please visit her online at

www.cassidykoconnor.com.

You can also find her on Facebook at

https://www.facebook.com/C.K.-OConnor-Author-101376192171379

OR

www.facebook.com/cassidykoconnorauthor

Hi, I'm Sheri Lyn. I live in Florida with the two loves of my life, my dog's Bailey and Boone. I love living here and couldn't imagine living anywhere else.

I'm an avid reader who kept dreaming of a story that wanted to be told and that's where my first book was born.

When I'm not reading or proofing, I'm at the evil day job where my sanity is tested on a daily basis. My sarcastic quips can provide a much-needed break until I can return home to my puppies and books, my joys in life.

Please visit my website to keep up with my books and to sign up for my newsletter for excerpts, give-aways and fun.

Sherilynauthor.com and on Twitter - @sherilynauthor

Sneak Peek of Stitched Under Fire

Chapter One

"This is Sicily Bronson with ABC Action News on the scene in Downtown Tampa where a paranormal fight resulted in catastrophic damage to humans and infrastructure. We have an eyewitness here to describe what happened."

"I saw the whole thing. I was sitting in the cafe over there drinking my coffee. That's when it all started. Darkness overtook the street, and the roars echoed down from above. The sound gave me goose-bumps all over my body. Then suddenly a long tail swooped down, barely missing a couple walking." The witness pointed to a spot on the other side of the road.

"The creatures were in a battle to the death and it was obvious they didn't care who they hurt in the process. The dragon, at least I think that's what it was. It looked nothing like they do in the movies. It dug its talons into the minotaur's back." The man imitated the claws wrapping around a large body.

"The minotaur screamed so loud the windows actually shattered, glass went everywhere. People were screaming as they got cut up from the flying shards. Next thing you know, the dragon had opened his claws, and the Minotaur was falling to the ground. That's when I saw the chunk of the leg missing from the minotaur."

The man paused as he blew out a breath and focused on a spot outside. "It crashed to the ground, crushing vehicles and smashing the windows of the buildings as it went. The dragon followed after it, blowing fire. That's when a small car turned down the road and slammed to a stop. The minotaur grabbed the dragon by the throat and pinned it to the street, blocking the car's path. I thought maybe it was over then, you know." He licked his lips as he glanced back at the reporter as tears filled his eyes.

"The dragon blew a fireball into the minotaur's face, sending him backward. Then they ran at each other as the dragon blew out another fireball. They crashed into one another and were thrown on top of the car. The dragon stood first, slamming its tail on top of the car, repeatedly trying to crush the minotaur. And then it was as if the whole world froze but for the screaming coming from inside the car. The dragon grabbed the minotaur in its claws and flew away with it. There was nothing left behind but silence."

"Well, I think everyone would agree we're glad to see you are safe." Sicily turned back to the camera. "There's a press conference scheduled later today with more details, but preliminary estimates are coming in with at least five dead, and another fifteen injured. The most critical patients were sent to Tampa Medical Center. The property damage is expected to reach the millions. We're told a manhunt is still underway for the responsible parties."

Chapter Two

Maddox grabbed the last gallon of paint out of Tristan's truck and hauled it inside.

Tallie, the teenage ex-prostitute currently staying with his mother, squealed as she saw the dab of color on the lid. "My room is going to be insane. You guys are the best."

She skipped down the hall. Maddox let out a deep breath.

"You guys spoil her, and I think that's awesome. She deserves to have the room she never had as a child." Marta, Maddox's mom, patted his shoulder affectionately.

He had to maintain an air of grumpiness, but deep inside, there was nothing he wouldn't do for the girl. If she wanted her room to look like she lived in an actual tree with a waterfall flowing around it, he would have found a way to make it happen. Lucky for them, she only asked for a forest mural. Tallie had grown up with an abusive father until she ran away to live on the streets. She didn't deserve the hand dealt to her. His mom offering to take the girl in to help with her own loneliness was the perfect fix.

"Hey, Marta," Tristan called out with a twinkle in his eye. "You know our new apartment isn't decorated yet. Your son is being no help with colors. I keep telling him he's gay, he should have a say, but he's as stubborn as the day is long. What's his favorite color?"

"He always loved fuchsia."

Maddox gagged. "Absolutely not. Nothing should ever be painted that shade of disgustingness. I will be so pissed if I come home and my living room is now that god awful color."

Tristan laughed. "I noticed you didn't specify if it was pink or purple. I swear some of those combinations confuse the hell out of me."

"Stop flirting and get in here and work on my room," Tallie yelled from down the hall with impatience.

"Geez, didn't take her long to get comfortable bossing us around," Maddox grumbled as he hustled down the hall.

"Something tells me with her former line of work she learned how to read what people like... as in you taking orders ...."

Maddox glared at him over his shoulder. "We both know there isn't a submissive bone in my body."

Tristan threw his head back in laughter as he trailed after his partner down the hall and into the teen's bedroom. "So... we didn't talk about this before, but I can't draw. And unless you're hiding that ability from me.... We may not have thought this through completely."

Maddox cocked his head as he stared at the empty wall. "Um Tallie, how good of a job are you expecting? If it ends up looking like a kindergarten class did it, would that be okay with you?"

"Grandma," Tallie screamed in alarm as she raced toward the door in wide-eyed terror.

Maddox bit back a grin. It sounded so weird to hear her call his mom grandma. It was sweet, but weird.

Marta popped her head in. "You already have a problem? You haven't even started."

Tallie waved her arms violently toward Maddox and Tristan. "These two agreed to the mural and just now admitted they can't actually draw."

Marta smiled broadly. "You know... your dad is a fantastic artist. What if he comes over and sketches it all out? All you guys have to do is paint between the lines."

Maddox's stomach did a little flip. His relationship with his dad was tenuous at best and his relationship with Tristan was still hovering around first base. Was he ready to have them meet?

Tristan's eyes bugged as he slowly raised his hand to gain their attention. "I'm not sure I'm ready to meet the 'rents. That's like a year long relationship milestone. Not like I met your son a couple of months ago and moved in together last week."

Marta cocked an eyebrow at him. "I'm a 'rent as you call it and you've already met me. I feel like chopped liver. You're only worried about meeting his dad?"

"No... well shit." He grumbled as he moved to hide behind Maddox. "That's so not how I meant that at all. But I can see where I went wrong. And now I'm just making it worse with my blabbering. Maddox, help me out here."

Maddox crossed his arms over his chest. "How dare you offend my mother, in her own house."

Tristan gaped at his sort of boyfriend. "You Judas. If we shared a room, I'd kick you to the couch for that."

Tallie gasped. "Oh my god. You guys sleep in separate rooms?"

Maddox looked at her, then over at his mom. This was not a conversation he wanted to have with either of them.

Marta held a hand up to stop him before he could respond. "As much as I too would love an answer to that question, I know better than to expect one from you. I'll call your dad and see when he's available."

"Your son has decided to take things slow with me. My virtue is intact I'll have you know."

Tallie scrunched her eyebrows together. "Wait, I thought Maddox was some kind of man-whore?"

Maddox rubbed his eyes. "This just keeps getting worse. Can I die now and avoid all of these conversations?" He sighed and looked back at Tallie. "Not that it's your business, but both of us had thirty-six plus years of prejudices and hatred to get past. He was a human six weeks ago. That's a big change on its own, let alone starting a relationship, too." He looked back at Marta. "Cover your ears for a second." He turned back to Tallie. "Trust me, I want to obliterate his virtue. I just thought taking it slow was good for him."

"And now I sound like I was complaining when I was only making a joke at your expense. But he's right Tallie. I'm not quite ready to go there yet. I've gone through some major upheavals and it's changed my whole world. That being said, I've been into guys since I knew what my dick was for. So I appreciate a gorgeous guy when I see one." He winked at her as he heard Marta snort from behind him.

Marta pulled out her phone. "I'm going to save my son from any further embarrassment and call his dad." She pulled out her cell and hit a button. "Silas, your son needs you. How soon can you be here?"

The air in the room thinned seconds before a portal opened and his dad stepped through. "I'm here. What's wrong?"

Every jaw in the room was open. Maybe he shouldn't be surprised his dad came so quickly, nevertheless, it shocked him. He didn't really have a relationship with him, so why would he come running to his aid?

Marta recovered first and slid her phone back in her pocket. "Well, that was efficient. Thank you for coming."

Maddox could swear her face was red. Ewww.

Silas scanned the room. "I think there are a few introductions that need to be made?"

Maddox pointed to Tallie first. "This is Tallie. She is a friend that needed a place to stay and mom offered to let her live with her for a while." Silas nodded at the girl then looked expectantly at Tristan. "This is, uh... Tristan... my partner."

"Partner on the force..." Tristan offered a wave and then winced... "Uh... and um... we just started dating, too." He grimaced and looked at Maddox. "I freaking panicked and didn't know what to say." He whispered loudly.

Silas walked up to Tristan and stood inches from him. For a long minute, he just stared at him. Maddox was about to intervene when Silas reached forward and gave Tristan a hug. "It is wonderful to meet you." He stepped back and over to Tallie. "And I suppose I'll be seeing a lot of you now that you're living here."

Maddox swung around to Marta. How often was his dad over for booty calls?

She definitely was blushing this time. "Anyway. We called you over because it turns out these two offered their services for something they can't even do."

Maddox's phone buzzed in his pocket. He saw the call was from Vic, their boss at P.I.S. "Excuse us a second." He waved at Tristan to follow him out into the hall.

Maddox answered and put the phone on speaker. "Hey Vic. What's up?"

"Remember when you called in the other day after the near destruction of Downtown Tampa and

I told you not to come in, we had it handled? Well, we just had a body drop that needs our attention. I know you two are off for another day, but I really need you to come in."

"Not a problem. You are saving us from a very awkward situation anyway. Be there in an hour." Maddox hung up the phone and popped his head back into the bedroom. "We got called into work so unfortunately we have to go. We can make plans to meet up again to work on the mural if you want?"

Silas was already drawing on one wall. "You two go ahead. Marta and Tallie are in excellent hands."

Maddox shuddered. Now that he knew his parents still hooked up, he was horrified on a whole new level. He was never so happy to go see a dead body.

Chapter Three

Tristan stayed quiet as they drove to the office. He couldn't get the morning out of his head, mainly meeting his partner's father and making an ass of himself. "Hey man. Why didn't you ever mention how fucking gorgeous your father was? I could have been so much smoother if I'd been forewarned. But no, he just popped in and I froze. He's a total Silver Fox."

"First of all, you knew he was Fae, so automatically it's a given they are good looking. Second, who says their parent is gorgeous? That's just weird. Do you say your mom is hot?"

"Uh, she might have been once upon a time. But time and her illness have taken a toll on her." Tristan shrugged as he pulled into a spot. "Is it wrong to say I can see why your mom has a thing for him? You take after him a bit though too."

"Am I going to have to keep you away from him? Do I need to worry about some daddy fetish you might act on?" Maddox shot back as he got out of the truck.

"Wait... is that a possibility? Does he bat for our team too?" Tristan held up his hands in an I surrender gesture and laughed. "Just kidding. I swear I was just teasing you. Trying to lighten the mood a bit."

Before Maddox could respond, Vic opened the door to their pod area with a folder already held out. "Glad you guys could dress for the occasion. We have a werewolf found in an alley in Ybor and I'll save what's special about it for when you guys get there."

Tristan looked down at his casual house work outfit, "We have a change of clothes in our office here. Figured we could kill two birds with one stone and stop here before going to the crime scene. If you want us to go home first, we can do that..."

Maddox pushed past them toward their office. "Dude Tristan. He's just giving you a hard time. Get your clothes, we'll check in with the team, then head out."

Vic smirked. "Do we need to have someone monitor the locker rooms while you guys change? Time is of the essence, after all."

"No worries there. We live together now. We can behave ourselves at work." Maddox smiled cheekily as he grabbed a gym bag from his desk.

Tristan groaned as he reached for his own tote. "Dude, stop saying shit like that to him. I don't care what relationship you have with him. It still freaks me out that he's our boss. I'm still the low man on the totem pole and I need this job."

Maddox ignored him and stopped at the table in the center of the pod. Ensley and Sheppard were staring at a laptop. "Hey guys. Any progress made on your case?"

Sheppard sat back and blew out a breath. "It's been eight days and we still don't have these assholes in custody. We've identified them, but they seem to have disappeared."

"We still have four people in critical condition, too. These guys really fucked up." Ensley said as she pushed away from the table to grab a pastry from a box behind her.

"Knowing who they are is something though, they can't hide forever. You'll get them." Tristan reassured them.

"Well, if you guys need someone to be a sounding board, let us know." Maddox held up the folder Vic had handed him. "In the meantime, it appears we got a mysterious body to go check out."

Ensley glared. "Oh sure, rub it in. You guys are going to do something fun."

Sheppard elbowed his partner. "That is so morbid."

Tristan nodded in agreement with him as he gestured to the door, "We gotta go change. We'll see you guys later."

Some days he really questioned the mental stability of people in this line of work.

Tristan and Maddox flashed their badges at the Tampa PD cop, then ducked under the police tape.

"I really hope Judd is the forensics tech on this one. You haven't met Bruce yet. Guy is a fox shifter and is just as shifty as a human. Judd is great though. Super nice and goes out of his way to help in any way he can."

The tech in question stood up and turned to wave them over. He held his hand out to Tristan. "We haven't met yet. I'm Judd."

Tristan smiled and accepted the handshake. "Hey."

Judd grinned, "I've heard a lot about you. Gossip runs rampant around the office. Add in that you've apparently tamed the untamable and you're already a legend."

"He got to you too?" Tristan groaned good-naturedly.

"Nope," Judd winked, "Actually, we're just friends. I knew his reputation before I joined P.I.S. and no matter how charming he is, I resisted. It was difficult, but I did it."

Maddox grunted, "You aren't even gay."

"Not necessarily, but I didn't slam that door closed. If the right person came along, who knows what would happen." Judd grinned and waved to an officer standing off to the side. "He was the first on the scene. We've already taken his statement. He didn't have much to offer, though. He claims not to have disturbed the scene or touched the body. There was no way the guy was alive, so he just called it in."

Tristan cocked his head. "Why were we called in over his forensics team? From here I can't tell that he's a paranormal."

"If you step to the side a bit, you'll see his hand has partially shifted." Judd explained as he pointed, "He moved back to the opening of the alley and kept it blocked until more units could arrive to hold the scene. It's basically been untouched until we arrived with Sabrina a few hours ago. We're actually getting ready to take the body once you guys have had your look around."

"Did you find anything of note?" Tristan asked as

he took in the markers littered around the dirty alley.

Judd laughed sarcastically, "It's impossible to tell what's of use and what's the usual garbage left here on a normal day." He turned and waved. "Sabrina, you have a minute?"

"This is our M.E. Dr. Sabrina Zanders. Doc, this is the agency's newest recruit, Tristan James."

Sabrina smiled and offered her hand. "Sorry we're meeting under these circumstances, but I've got to tell you, this is one odd case."

"Yeah, Vic mentioned there was something weird about this one," Maddox mentioned as he walked closer to the body.

"You could say that. We won't know everything until we get him back, but it appears the only thing wrong with him besides most of his blood being on the outside of his body is that it looks like his kidneys are gone. You can see two incisions on either side of the abdomen."

"I'm sorry. Did you say his kidneys are missing?" Maddox bent down and looked closer at the gashes.

"Neat right? You hear about this stuff on T.V. but I've never actually had a case like this." Judd said a little excitedly.

Tristan was going to add him to the list with Ensley and their questionable mental stability.

"The time of death was between four and eight a.m. yesterday. I'll do an autopsy immediately and let you know what else I find." Sabrina nodded at them and walked away.

"Did he have a wallet or anything to identify him?" Tristan asked Judd as he squatted down to get a better look at the body and the surrounding area.

"Yes, it's bagged up already. His name is Mark Sequoia. He lived a couple of blocks from here according to the address on his license." Judd handed over the evidence bag. "That's all I know so far."

Tristan nodded and stood up. "You seen enough?"

"Yeah, let's get back and start looking into who might want to kill Mr. Sequoia."

"Hey Judd, can you send us the photos you guys have taken as soon as you can?" Tristan requested as he glanced around one more time.

"Sure thing. We'll be bagging the body in a moment and then I'll get them uploaded to the system so you guys can access them by the time you get back to the office."

Tristan paused and turned back to face Judd.

"Who took the officer's statement? Has anyone set up a canvas of the area?"

"Tampa PD is handling that part. The officer's statement is already written up and uploaded as well. We were on scene for a bit before you guys were sent out. We were just waiting for you to see the scene before we finished up."

Maddox shook Judd's hand. "You're a rockstar as always. See you later." He caught up to Tristan on the way out of the alley. "You know... Mrs. Diaz's food truck is two streets over. We can get some lunch to take back to the office?"

Tristan's stomach growled at the thought of her delicious food. "Hell yes. It's a date."

"Speaking of dates. We need to go on a real one soon. I'm free tonight if you are?"

"You don't know my schedule? It's not like I've been far from your side since the day we met." Tristan laughed and shook his head. "The only thing I have planned any time soon is going to visit my mom. It's been a few days since I saw her." He hesitated. "You're welcome to come with me sometime if you want. She's not always lucid enough to know me, but some days I get lucky."

Maddox mock gasped. "I thought it was too soon

to meet the 'rents." His smile dropped. "In all seriousness, though. I would love to meet her."

"Don't worry, she'll love you. Anyone that has her baby boy's back is good in her book."

Maddox reached across the truck cab and pinched Tristan's cheek. "Oh, her baby boy. That is freaking adorable. I'd ask if I can start calling you baby boy, but I really don't want to feed into that daddy fetish."

To continue reading purchase *Stitched Under Fire* now.

www.ingramcontent.com/pod-product-compliance
Lightning Source LLC
Chambersburg PA
CBHW070629260626
47161CB00007B/2636